Ian didn't say anything more; just bundled up her wrapped purchases, took her money and handed back her change. It wasn't until she was walking out the door, those out-of-place boots clunking against the floor with each step, that he realized he wasn't going to see her again.

"Miss Ella?" She turned expectantly, and he lifted himself to his foot. "If you need anything else, I'd be happy to help you." He meant *if you need anything else to buy* but when her lips curled up again, he realized he'd help her with anything else she needed, too.

"Thank you, Mr. Crowne."

"Ian." He adjusted his glasses, more for something to do with his hands than a real need.

A slight nod, and those turquoise-blue eyes raked his shoulders and his forearms again. He watched her tongue dart out and swipe her upper lip, and knew that the sight was going to haunt him tonight. "Ian." His name was low and delicious on her lips, and he figured he wasn't going to get any sleep at all, imagining her saying his name over and over again.

And then she was gone, and Manny barked once. Ian sank down on his stool again, and dropped his hand to the dog's head to scratch. "You and me both, lad," he muttered.

Maybe she was special.

Cissie

Ella

An Everland Ever After Tale

Thanks for the
Love & Support

Caroline Lee ♡

Caroline

The Sweet Cheyenne Quartet

Caroline Lee

A Cheyenne Christmas
A Cheyenne Celebration
A Cheyenne Thanksgiving
A Cheyenne Christmas Homecoming
Where They Belong: A Sweet Cheyenne Christmas
Novella

Dedication:

For the Pioneer Hearts readers and authors who have formed the most welcoming group in the Wild Wild Web...

Everyone else really should join us there!

First edition: 2016

This work is made available in e-book format by Amazon Kindle at
www.amazon.com
And in paperback format by CreateSpace at www.createspace.com

Printing/manufacturing information for this book may be found on the last
page

Cover: EDHGraphics

Once Upon a Time...

The little girl huddled against her mother in the wagon. It wasn't cold, but as they were ferried across the empty plains, she needed the reassurance her mother's comforting presence brought. "Will my new papa like me, Mama?"

Mama smiled down at her. "How could he not, Ella? You're sweet and helpful and will be a good daughter to him. I told him all about you—what a good little seamstress you are—in my letters."

Just as he'd written all about his daughters. "Will my new sisters like me?"

"Of course they will. Having sisters is the most wonderful bond in the world, and I'm so glad that you're finally going to have some." She'd had a baby brother once, but he'd died a long time ago, before her Papa did. But now, Mama was going to remarry, and she was going to have *three* sisters.

It was very exciting. And terrifying.

"Will I like living on a ranch, Mama?"

"I hope so, sweetheart." This time, Mama's voice sounded less sure. "Your new Papa is a wealthy man. He has hundreds and hundreds of cattle, and can afford nice things for his daughters." She gave the girl a little squeeze. "His girls need a Mama, just like we need a new home. I'm excited to meet him." The quaver in her voice told the girl that Mama was nervous too, so she hugged her back.

Before long, the livery wagon crested a ridge, and the two of them saw their new home; a large house surrounded by outbuildings and gardens and activity. The mountains in the distance lent a sort of stark beauty to the place, and mother and daughter shared a smile.

Those smiles grew when they saw their new family waiting for them in front of the house. The imposing, serious-looking man cradling the curious toddler must be her new Papa. She watched as Mama greeted him awkwardly, and decided that she would reserve judgement on him.

But much more intriguing were the two girls standing haughtily beside him. One was her age, and one a little older. All three girls had the palest blonde hair she ever did see, in sharp contrast to her own dark curls.

"Hello! I'm Ella!" Mama had taught her to be polite, and she was excited to start her friendship with her new sisters.

The older one sniffed haughtily and looked away. "Eunice, she looks like an Indian. Or a Gypsy, maybe. Check to see if she's wearing any shoes."

Ella knew that her clothing wasn't as nice as her new sisters', but she hadn't expected insults. At a loss, she watched the other girl bend over to peek at her naked feet, and self-consciously tucked her toes under her skirt.

Eunice, the chubby girl her own age, straightened and smiled good-naturedly. "Nope, Mabel." But then she nodded at Ella. "That's okay, though. You can borrow some of mine. We have millions of dresses and shoes."

"She can borrow some of *yours*, if you think you can *trust* her."

Ella had to defend herself. "You can trust me! We're sisters now!"

"Quiet down, girls." Her new Papa's harsh censure surprised Ella, and made her blush in embarrassment at being caught losing her temper so early. She peeked up at her new Papa, but he was speaking quietly to Mama, making her blush as well. Ella wondered why.

She didn't have to wonder long, though, before Papa thrust the littlest blonde sister in her arms. "Here you go, girl. Carry Sibyl while I show your mother around my house."

As he led Mama away, Eunice and Mabel flouncing in his wake, Mama turned around once to gaze at Ella. The girl forced a smile on her face to reassure her mother, as she struggled to support the beautiful little toddler in arms that were not used to the task.

When Mama turned back to the house, Ella suddenly felt a warm wetness creeping across her tummy. She looked at Sibyl, sucking beatifically on one thumb, and realized what had happened.

Her new sister had peed on her.

CHAPTER ONE

Wyoming Territory, 1875

At least no one was kicking her awake.

Ella woke quickly, as was her habit, but took the time to relish that quiet moment before the sun lightened the kitchen enough to justify her getting up. There had been mornings—none recently, thank the Lord—that she'd overslept, and had been woken by angry screeches about breakfast and gowns and hairstyles.

But not today.

After not nearly enough moments enjoying the comfort of her blankets, the sun crested the Wyoming hills and hit the small mirror she'd positioned in the window for just this purpose. The beam of reflected light hit the pillow by her head, and she sighed. Time to get up.

The kitchen had been her home for eight years, since her mother had died and Mabel convinced Papa that she needed her own room. So Eunice moved in with Sibyl, and Ella… well, there weren't enough beds for Ella, so she made do with the warmth of the fireplace in the kitchen. At least here, she was safe from their cruelty. Mostly.

Folding away her pallet and blankets, Ella slipped on the light slippers Papa insisted that she wear in the house, and listened to the sounds of the birds. They would often come and perch on the windowsill and trill at her early in the morning, no matter how often she tried to shoo them away. In the summer heat, the window was wide open, and it was only a matter of time before that particularly loud lark showed up to sing at her. They had a way of knowing when she was working, and Ella — completely baffled by the whole thing — had long ago resigned herself to their company.

She set a pot of water to boil on the stove, knowing that Papa and her stepsisters liked their coffee first thing, and then tied an apron around her dress — she only had the two — and got to work washing and peeling potatoes for breakfast.

The outside door opened and closed, and Ella heard Maisie's happy humming. The older woman lived with her husband in a little cabin on the far side of the barns, and she joined Ella each morning to cook the food for the ranch hands' morning meal. The two of them were friends… or as close of friends as Papa would let her be with a former slave.

"You get the eggs from this morning already?"

The other woman held up her basket, her eyes twinkling. "Those chickens listen to me better'n your birds listen to you." She carefully balanced the basket on the shelf above the counter, and began to roll up her own sleeves.

"*Listen* to me? Those birds don't even know I'm here." She moved the potatoes to the board and got out the good knife, careful to keep her fingertips out of the way.

"*Hmmmm.* You think they coming here to visit *me*? Nah, them animals like just you."

"I don't see why," Ella grumbled. "I don't like them." From the corner of her eye, she watched a brown shape scurry out from behind one of the stones in the hearth. She'd long ago stopped screaming when the mice scampered across her pillow, but now she glared down at this one's big beady eyes. It somehow managed to look pleading, and Ella didn't have the time to chase it away. With an exasperated eye-roll, she flicked a chunk of potato off the counter, and pretended not to hear Maisie's chuckle when the bothersome little pest took her pity-offering and scampered off.

"I can't imagine why they'd like you." Maisie laid on the sarcasm thick enough to chew, and Ella tossed a potato piece at her. It bounced off the center of the dark woman's forehead, and landed on the floor, where the mouse scooped *it* up too. Neither woman could stifle their giggles when the creature ran back to its den with double the bounty.

Ella cut the bacon while Maisie fried the first batch for the cowboys, and they chatted. "Have you been out to see the puppies?"

"Only one left, now."

"Oh, no. The mama still hasn't come back?"

"Nope, but Leonard says this girl's strong, and she'll make it fine. He says a few of the other men been acting interested in her too, so maybe he'll have some help keepin' her strong." Ella smiled at the good news. "Of course, she likes you best of all. Just like them birds and mice and —"

Maisie screeched when Ella pretended to threaten her with the big knife, and they both dissolved into giggles again.

They fell into companionable silence, each used to the other's presence during the rush of breakfast preparation. Ella had the coffee done, the potatoes fried, and the eggs cooking in the bacon drippings when the first creaks came from overhead. Both women turned to look at the ceiling, and then at each other.

"Miss Mabel's up early."

Ella hummed noncommittedly, hurrying in her tasks. Years ago, it had been her duty—Mabel had *made* it her duty—to get her stepsisters dressed in the morning. Then, when she'd taken over the cooking for the family, Mabel had bullied Sibyl into helping her and Eunice. But they were fast dressers, and if they were up, then Papa was probably already in the dining room.

She pulled off the apron, settled everything on the tray, and turned to find Maisie giving her a sympathetic look. "You want me to help you carry all of that?"

Ella smiled thankfully. "And let you take some of the credit for this fine meal?" Her teasing made the other woman smile, as she'd known it would. "No ma'am. I've got to butter them all up."

"Today's the day you going into town?"

"Mabel wants a new dress for the July Fourth parade and picnic, so of course the other girls demanded one, too. I've got to go find some more white ribbon and lace, if there's any left. Papa's got to let me go."

Maisie smiled sadly and patted her arm. "They worked your mama to death, and now work you too hard too, child."

That caused a slight laugh. "Of course they do. But if these dresses are pretty enough, maybe they'll all find beaus — finally! — and get married and go away and leave me alone."

"Your sisters are ugly inside, and the men 'round these parts know it." Ella noticed that Maisie's voice had dropped to a whisper, lest Edmund Miller hear her insult his precious daughters. "They ain't gettin' married 'til they change their ways."

"Hush that nonsense, Maisie. They've *got* to get married; I'm not going to escape them otherwise!"

"You could always find yourself a man. You're a pretty girl, inside and out. Find a handsome prince and ride away from here."

Ella burst into laughter, not quite sure if her friend was teasing. "And where would I find a man around here?" She shook her head, still smiling, while she rolled down her sleeves and made sure that her dark curls were contained in a neat bun. Mabel and Eunice gave her enough trouble for not having straight blonde hair like they did; Ella tried her hardest to keep from looking "slovenly," which always set them off. "And even if I did, why would I want to leave all of this?" She swept one hand around the room in mock seriousness, gesturing at the kitchen's tight space and inadequate light and vermin-infested hearth.

Maisie relented, and smiled at her teasing. "All right, go on then. Go serve them bullies you call your sisters, and then go have fun in town."

"I will!" she called as she backed through the door to corridor, her arms full with the silver tray that had belonged to Papa's mother back in Boston.

Sure enough, her stepfather was sitting at his spot at the head of the table, reading yesterday's *Wyoming Tribune*. He ignored her as she poured his coffee, and only glanced up when his own daughters came stampeding into the room, making much to-do about sitting down and serving themselves. Ella served herself last, of course, and settled at the far end of the table, next to her mother's empty place.

It wasn't far into the meal before her sisters were bickering with each other over who was wearing whose jewelry. Ella kept her head down, hoping they wouldn't turn their ire on her. She'd learned soon after coming to the Miller Ranch that her sisters—and even her stepfather—didn't need an excuse to rail at her. As always, Papa kept his attention on his paper; Ella suspected that it was less out of fascination with the news, and more out of a desire to ignore his daughters.

But by the end of the meal, she couldn't avoid drawing their attention. "Excuse me, Papa?"

"Hmmmm…?" He frowned a bit when he realized that it was his stepdaughter who'd interrupted his breakfast ritual.

"I was wondering…" Ella swallowed and hurried through her explanation. "Once I've completed my chores, may I go into town? I need some new trim for my sister's dresses."

As expected, Papa's frown grew—he never allowed her into town, not even for church services—and her sister protested.

"Absolutely not! Papa, she hasn't waxed the bannister yet!"

"I wanted her to stitch the holes in my stockings today!"

"You can't go! You promised you'd finish my curtains!"

Rather than addressing her stepsisters' whining, Ella kept her expression calm, and faced Papa. He rarely looked right at her, and today was no exception. She felt like he was scowling at a spot on the wall behind her, but she folded her hands in her lap and straightened her spine, as Mama had taught her. "I can't finish Sibyl's curtains without the lace I was planning on buying today, and I finished stitching Eunice's stocking yesterday." She refused to let herself glance at her spoiled sisters. "And I stayed up late waxing the bannister last night. The house is clean, and I'll be back before dinner."

"If all you need is some lace, girl, have Maisie or one of the hands pick some up next time they're in town." Her stepfather's voice was still as strong as it used to be, when he'd call her a stupid, lazy girl. Ella felt the muscles along her jaw tighten, and forced herself to remain calm.

"Your daughters have already picked out their material, and I'm half-complete with the dresses for the big celebration. I'm sorry, but I don't trust anyone else to choose the right colors of trim that will go with the fabric. I won't know what to get until I see what is available."

She held her breath, hoping that he'd say yes, but knowing it was a long shot. "I hardly think that the task is too difficult—"

She played her ace. "I would hate to think of my sisters being forced to wear uncoordinated dresses."

There was a chorus of slight gasps, and then all three spoke at once.

"You *must* let her go, Papa!"

"Only Ella can choose the right colors. You *know* that she has an eye for such things."

"Pass the bacon, please."

Ella hid her smile as Mabel scowled at the middle Miller sister. "*More* bacon? Ella will have to let out your dress before the picnic."

Eunice shrugged. "Just so long as the trim matches that lovely green silk I picked out." She took a big bite of bacon and pinned her father with an expectant stare.

When faced with three sets of ice-blue eyes—identical to his own—Edmund Miller sighed, and gestured to his stepdaughter. "Fine. Fine. I'll tell Heyward that he's to have one of the men spell him, and he'll accompany you. But you'll make sure that all of your work is done before you leave, and you'll be back by dinner."

Well, of course I will. No one else will cook it for you. But Ella just smiled tightly and said "Yes, Papa" and tried not to let her stepsisters see how pleased she was, as she cleaned up the breakfast dishes. She knew that they'd find a way to stop her little excursion, if they knew how badly she wanted to go.

Going to town! When was the last time she'd been? Ella honestly couldn't remember. Since Mama's death, Papa had insisted that she stay here on the ranch, and he set guards to make sure that she didn't leave. Her stepsisters claimed that it was because she was so ugly that he wanted everyone to forget he married her mother, and forget about her. Ella figured that it was more likely because if she stayed out of town and out of the townspeople's memory, there was no one to keep her from cooking and cleaning and slaving for him and his spoiled daughters. It got lonely, but with no one in town to miss — and no one to miss her — it didn't much matter.

But Ella hadn't been lying to her family; she really did need to be the one to pick out the trimmings for these particular dresses. Her sisters had ordered the fashion magazines, and picked out the material themselves on their twice-weekly trips into Everland. She'd been slaving over the three dresses for weeks now.

These three gowns had to be *perfect.* This was the year, she vowed. The year that her creations finally got Eunice and Mabel noticed by *some* man, and married. They were desperate to be courted, and Ella was desperate to get them out of her hair. At nineteen and twenty-one, they were the belles of the area — to hear Sibyl tell it while her sisters preened. But so far no young beaus had stepped forward.

This year, Ella planned to make them gorgeous, elaborate dresses, and fill their picnic baskets with as many delicious concoctions as she could manage. Some man in the Everland area would bid on their baskets and start courting her sisters, or she'd pull her own hair out.

Ella *would* get her stepsisters married, by God.

Everland had certainly grown since the last time she'd been to town. Of course, that'd been several years ago, and only to buy new slippers, so it was no wonder that no one recognized her. She didn't recognize any of them, and just barely remembered the layout of some of the shops. With the railroad spur, hundreds of new people must come through Everland each year, and the town had expanded accordingly.

Unfortunately, though, the stores were having trouble keeping up with the rush. With the Independence celebration so near, the mercantiles had been picked over. Both shops she'd visited that morning had only a few fabric trimmings left. She'd picked up a lovely half-bolt of white lace for Mabel's pale pink confection—Papa spared no expense when it came to his princesses—but she still needed something for Sibyl and a fringe for Eunice.

There was one place left to try. Mrs. Pedlar over at the dry goods store had reluctantly sent her this way, saying that she didn't think there'd be any good fabric at all here, because the owner was a man, and what did he know? But Ella was desperate; she wasn't likely to get another trip into Everland.

So now she stood in the dusty street in her sturdy boots, looking up at the porch in front of the little storefront. The hand-painted sign proudly proclaimed it "Crowne's Mercantile" and there

were three dogs stretched out on the wooded
boards. One — a shaggy mountain of an animal —
panted in the heat, but the other two appeared to
be sleeping. As she stepped onto the porch, though,
they all lifted their heads, and one of them whined
slightly.

Mr. Heyward spit a stream of tobacco juice
onto the dirt road behind her, and Ella winced at
his disgusting manners. Her stepfather's right-
hand man had ridden into town beside her on his
imposing black horse — which kept trying to nudge
her for some reason — and had been following her
around to the stores, waiting outside. She hated the
man, and for more than just his casual cruelty and
his lewd smirks. She hated him because he was
always the one who Papa set to watching her, if she
had to be out of the house. Having him beside her
was the ultimate proof of her stepfather's power
over her life, and *that's* why she really hated him.

But at least Papa had let her come to town,
even if it did mean putting up with Mr. Heyward's
lewd smirks, bad breath, embarrassingly naughty
jokes, and the way he was always looking at her
like she was some kind of tasty morsel. She was
having an adventure, by Heaven, and nothing he
could do was going to hamper that.

The door to the shop was open to catch the
breeze, so she lifted her chin and stepped through.
Inside, Crowne's was neat and tidily organized and
filled to the brim with goods. There were ropes
strung tautly across the room about seven feet up,
being used as a sort of advertisement, with goods
dangling off of them. Barrels overflowed with nails
and flour and pickles, and there were tins of food
and folded piles of ready-made clothes and bolts of

cloth. Ella gave a little sigh of relief when she saw how many were there—surely there'd be trim to go with it?

She made a beeline for the table with the fabric, and had to move some of the bolts out of the way. There was flannel and denim and cotton and silk, but that was it. She didn't see any lace or embellishments *any*where! Ella made a little sound of frustration.

"Can I help you find something?"

She glanced towards the counter, intended to wave away the offer, but when her brain caught up with her eyes, she stopped mid-movement. Frankly, it was remarkable that her jaw didn't drop.

There, behind the counter, was one of the most attractive men she'd ever seen. He had rust-colored hair neatly combed back, and a lovely dark vest, and glasses perched on a straight, regal nose. A regal nose? Where had that thought come from? Ella would've scoffed at herself, if she could stop gaping long enough to do so. The man had been working in a ledger, but now straightened, and she could see the sprinkling of light hair at the base of his neck where his collar fell open.

Most remarkable of all, though, was his size; his shoulders looked like they might break through the seams of his fine white shirt, and his sleeves were rolled up almost to his elbows in this heat, revealing powerful-looking forearms. Had she always found forearms so compelling? Right now, she couldn't remember. Couldn't remember *ever* seeing a set of forearms so fascinating.

"Miss?" She could hear the laughter in his voice, and would respond, just as soon as she could breathe again. "Can I help you find something in particular?"

"Lace." Ella managed to choke out the word, and watched him smile in response. Dear God, his *smile*. He had even white teeth, and were those… were those freckles? He had freckles? My, was it warm in here?

"Certainly. What kind do you need?" Her paragon pulled his glasses off to swipe at them with a handkerchief he'd pulled from his pocket. He had green eyes. But not just *any* green. Ella clamped down hard on her tongue, trying to stop her silly brain for waxing poetic about a pair of eyes, no matter how exquisite they might be.

By turning her attention back to the bolts of material, by touching them instead of his forearms, she was able to get her heart pounding normally again. A deep breath, and then: "I need trimmings for some dresses I'm working on. The other stores' supplies have been picked over, and I was hoping…" She swallowed. She was hoping for a lot.

She was hoping that Crowne's Mercantile carried lace and fringe. She was hoping that Mabel and Eunice would get married this year and move out. She was hoping that her sisters' ugly bullying would stop, and maybe she could be allowed to live her life in peace. She was hoping that Mr. Heyward would sprain his ankle and have to stop following her around. She was hoping that she'd be allowed back into town more regularly. She was hoping the gorgeous store-keeper would come over here and she might get to touch him, somehow.

Looks like she was going to get one of her wishes, at least. From the corner of her eye, she watched him settle his glasses back in place, brace both strong hands on the counter, and straighten further. He'd been perched on a high stool, and now that he stood, she realized just how tall he really was. With an odd little hop, he came around the corner of the counter, and then reached up to grab one of the ropes strung across the store. It wasn't until he hopped to the next table, holding the rope for balance and bracing his right hand on the displays of merchandise, that Ella looked down.

His right trouser leg—dark and pressed and neat—was pinned below his knee. She swallowed the hot taste in her throat, not sure why this injury would bother her more than the others she'd seen and read about in the decade since the war had ended. Was it because he was so young and handsome otherwise? How remarkable, that he'd been able to overcome the loss of a limb, and still manage this thriving store!

He swung to a stop beside her, and Ella forced her gaze up his body—his very well-built body—up to his face. And immediately felt guilty. Whereas, behind the counter, his expression had been open and welcoming, now he wore a carefully blank look. This close, she could see that his eyes were really a pale blue-green, but were now hooded, his brows tight and his jaw hard.

He'd caught her looking. Well, how could he not? She'd all but been gaping at him from the moment she saw him, and then had stared at his missing leg. She wondered what he'd seen on her face in that moment, and wondered why she felt so guilty about it. Swallowing, Ella offered him a sickly smile. "I'm sorry." Sorry for staring. Sorry for making him lose that gorgeous grin. Sorry for his injury.

This time his smile was tight and forced, looking like he was humoring her. A pale comparison to the way his face had lit up when he was laughing at her earlier. "Lace, you said?"

He was all business now. Dropping his hold on the rope, he shifted his hold on the table, canted his right leg out behind him for balance, and bent to reach for a half-hidden basket. Pulling it out from under the table, he hoisted it on top of two bolts of cotton, and Ella sucked in a breath at the way his muscles worked under the skin of those large forearms. No wonder his upper body was so well-built; he had to compensate for the loss of his foot and leg.

She could probably stand there all day, watching him pull smaller bolts from the basket, but he laid out a twist of white lace, as if waiting for her to inspect it. Intently aware of his heat beside her, his compelling bare forearm nearly touching her, Ella smoothed one finger down the white lace, ashamed of the dirt under her nails.

"Thank you." Hear voice caught, and she had to clear her throat. "Thank you, but I picked up something similar this morning." Hesitantly, she tilted her chin towards him, ready to stare back down at the lace again if he rebuffed her attempt at reconciliation. "Do you have anything else?"

Without answering, he tipped the basket over, spilling out the frills and ribbons and trimmings, and then turned back towards the counter. Ella busied herself pawing through the pile—so different from the ordered structure around her—but she wasn't really looking at it. No, she was seeing a pair of pale blue-green eyes flickering with disappointment at her rudeness.

With a sigh, Ella squeezed her eyes shut, resisting the urge to pinch the bridge of her nose. She flicked her gaze towards the counter again, seeing him bracing his weight on it while he hopped around the edge back towards his seat. Just when she'd thought her stomach couldn't sink any further, she realized that he'd created this mess for her, and would have to get back over here later to clean it up.

Straightening her shoulders, Ella told herself that just wasn't possible. She'd neaten up here. Focused now on her task, she examined each piece, roll, and bolt of embellishment, putting aside the ones with possibilities, and placing all the others neatly back into the basket.

Soon, she'd picked out a pretty white ribbon for Eunice's green silk. Her middle stepsister wouldn't like the plainness of it, but Ella could pair it with a few yards of *this* thick white fringe, and Eunice probably wouldn't even notice it. Without the ribbon to tie the decorations together, the fringe would look out of place… but her stepsisters really only cared about the ostentatious aspects of a dress. And judging from the size and quality of this ribbon, it'd cost Papa a pretty penny—which of course was no issue, as far as they were concerned—and thus would satisfy her stepsisters.

The ribbon would work for Sibyl's dress as well, but Ella continued to dig through the pile, just to marvel at the different textures and colors. At the very bottom, she found the most beautiful black velvet ribbon. It didn't go with any of the Miller sisters' gowns, but it was gorgeous. Ella held the bolt in one hand and stroked the ribbon across her opposite palm, quelling a delicious shiver at its softness against her skin.

Had she ever worn anything so decadent? She'd spent a decade sewing for her sisters, all manner of dresses and gowns for their weekly social outings and monthly suppers. Mabel and Eunice probably had a hundred dresses, between the two of them, and Ella had made all but a few of them. But none for herself. Ella had two dresses, an extra skirt, and a blouse. All of which had once belonged to her sisters, and were even plainer than their nightgowns. She wore her blue cotton in the summer, and her gray wool in the winter, and hoped that she found time to stitch up any rips or tears.

But *this*, this velvet… Ella sighed again, allowing it to caress her palm one more time. This was like a rich promise of… of… excitement and beauty and adventure.

And you'll never have the chance to wear it, she reminded herself sternly. Making quick work of rolling up the velvet ribbon, Ella gathered the spool of white ribbon and the fringed bolt, and turned to the counter.

And stopped short. He was smiling again. At *her*.

CHAPTER TWO

Ian watched the girl's concentration melt
into a look of wonder as she slowly stroked the
black ribbon, and he smiled. When she'd entered
his store—when she'd gazed at him like he was a
chocolate cake with cream and berries on top—
she'd looked every inch a woman. An *interested*
woman. But now, seeing the way her face
softened and her eyes went all hazy, Ian thought
she looked younger. More innocent.

And, as he settled back on his stool, he
had to admit that he liked her better this way. He
was used to women looking at him like she had at
first, seeing his broad shoulders and fine suits.
But as soon as they got a look at his leg—or
rather, where his leg had been—their expressions
inevitably all changed to pity. Every single one of
them.

Just like this girl's had. Oh, he hadn't
needed to be looking into those bright blue eyes
to see the pity there—he'd known it from the
small gasp she probably hadn't even noticed, and
the way her lips had tightened.

If he'd been smart, Ian would've just
stayed behind the counter, enjoying this
stranger's brief admiration, and pointed to the

basket of fripperies. But he'd long ago promised himself that he wasn't going to let his injury stop him from doing every single thing that a shop-owner should, and that included waiting on his customers.

Using his crutch in the store, however, was just silly; he hated having to maneuver around the displays. Instead, ropes ran around the store—he could use them for advertising, too—which he relied on for balance. Most of his customers had gotten used to seeing him hopping and shuffling and lifting himself around the store, but with the influx of people from the railway, he always got some stares.

He could swallow down the anger their pity left him feeling, and smile politely to make sales, because that's what mercantile owners did. They made sales. And judging from the amount of ribbon and whatnot this girl was collecting, he was about to make a big one.

So he was still smiling when she finally turned to him, her arms full of rolls and spools. And stopped dead. The look of surprise and bemusement crept back over her face, and Ian's smile grew. Yeah, maybe he was teasing her a little, but it shouldn't matter. She couldn't hide her pity at his leg; he wasn't going to hide him amusement at the way she stared.

But almost a minute went by before he finally broke the spell. "Miss…?

"Ella." That was definitely a blurt. She blurted out her name, and Ian hid his chuckle by clearing his throat.

"Nice to meet you, Ella." Although they hadn't officially "met", that didn't seem to bother her. "I'm Ian Crowne."

"This is your store?" Her dark brows went up, and he wondered if she was impressed.

A nod, and Ian didn't bother to hide his pride. "It is, indeed. Almost three years now, one of Everland's staples." She didn't need to know that it was a struggle to maintain the place by himself through the summer rushes, or to make enough through the long winter months.

Almost hesitantly, she picked her way toward his counter. Each footfall made a heavy *clu-clunk*, and Ian's trained eye picked out the boots—the kind the cowboys wore—peeking out from her worn blue dress. It was an odd choice of footwear for such a delicate little thing, but maybe she had a reason for wearing them. He'd heard from one of his regulars that the upcoming celebration had drawn a bunch of strangers—mysterious and otherwise—into town. And if she was coming through on the train—he'd definitely never seen her before—then maybe the footwear made sense.

He was thinking about the possibilities of ordering a few sets of sturdy boots for the women coming through when the girl dropped her purchases on the counter in front of him. He glanced up from them to find her smiling shyly, and he cursed himself for the sudden thickness in his throat—and his trousers. She was just a girl, passing through, who pitied him.

Still, he'd spent most of his life selling people things. "This ribbon will be lovely on you." He might not have many young women who shopped at his store yet, but he knew that compliments always worked. "For a dress you're making?"

She blushed. She actually blushed, and looked away, pretending great interest in a jar of hard candies. Ian studied her profile; skin pale enough that her cheeks pinked prettily, high cheekbones, a bottom lip a man might want to suck on, all capped with a head of black-as-coal hair. She'd pulled the mass of it back, but enough tendrils escaped around her forehead, ears and nape to prove that it was long and wavy. He'd always liked women with dark hair, and decided that—whatever her thoughts on him—he didn't mind looking at Ella one bit.

"It's not for me." Her admission was almost a whisper.

"You're a seamstress then?" That was a useful profession for a woman looking to start a new life out west—or wherever the train was taking her. Or maybe she was one of the unknown newcomers who were camped outside of town, and was hoping to one day set up shop here in Everland? He wouldn't mind seeing her more often.

"Of… Of sorts, I suppose." If he hadn't been staring at her, he might've missed the flash of blue when she peeked at him; because he didn't, Ian smiled gently and was rewarded with another blush. His chest puffed, thinking that he made a pretty girl blush. That was a feather in any man's cap, cripple or no.

Her hands fiddled with the ribbon, so he picked up the small bolt of fringe. "How much of this do you need?"

"Um…" Her finger skimmed over the ribbon gently, reverently. There were calluses on that finger, which Ian hadn't expected to see. A seamstress would have scars on her fingertips — his own mother had been one, and he remembered the way she'd her fingers would be poked with needles and pins while making dresses for her clients — but not full calluses. Perhaps they were from her journey westward? "All of it, I think. Just to be safe."

It was a smart idea, to buy it all so that she wouldn't run out; after all, when the train left tomorrow morning she'd be unable to return to buy more. But the businessman in him was pleased to hear the amount. "Excellent." He began to wrap the small bolt of fringe in brown paper. "Whatever you're making will certainly be lovely. I'm glad that I had enough for you."

She glanced up at him, and when she saw that he was smiling, relaxed a little. That same callused finger tucked a few strands of hair behind her ear as she shifted her weight from one hip to the other. "Honestly, you were my last stop, Mr. Crowne. Mrs. Pedlar told me that since this shop was run by a man, you were unlikely to have the right fripperies." Ian wasn't surprised; he had very few female customers, and assumed it was because of gossip. Pedlar Dry Goods was run by a husband and wife, with almost-grown children, so they had no end of help, and apparently most of the customers too. It was galling.

Ella continued airily, obviously not realizing the importance of her little confession. "But she must tell all the women that, because her fabrics were well-picked over."

"Not mine, though." He felt a little silly, defending his store to this stranger who was passing through, but it was instinctive. He wanted her to think well of him.

"Not yours." A smile, and Ian's breath caught. Had she been pretty when she was staring at him in awe, or when she blushed? When she smiled brightly like this, she was downright beautiful.

He felt the thickness climb up his throat again—the way it always did when he was attracted to a woman who would only pity him—and build in his trousers, and this time he didn't tamp it down. He was too busy looking, admiring, wondering at Ella's bright smile.

It was like a ray of sunshine had sneaked in through the door and wound its way around to the back of the store. Ian's heart felt *lighter*, somehow, staring at her. She was stunning.

And then something *did* sneak in through the door. Manny had been out on the porch with Shiloh and Vick, but he tended to not stay in any one place too long. Now he did his little hop-shuffle towards the counter, and caught Ella's attention. And she smiled again, when she saw the scrawny crippled dog. "Hello there. Who're you?"

She squatted down, right there in the middle of his store, and put her hand out for Manny to smell. The dog whined, and if he'd still had a tail, would've tucked in between his legs. Ian whistled quietly, and Manny's haunches lowered trustingly. As he lifted himself around the edge of the counter, Ian spoke to Ella. "This is Manny." The dog's tongue lolled out when he heard his name. "He's not fond of strangers."

Still with her hand out, Ella patiently smiled. "Hello Manny, I'm Ella." The dog took a cautious shuffle forward on its three legs, until he could sniff at Ella's hand. "See? Now we're not strangers, are we? Good boy, Manny." By the end of her soothing chatter, the dog let her scratch under his chin.

Ian, who'd been in the process of lowering himself down to assure Manny that Ella wouldn't hurt him, was surprised. Manny didn't often tolerate anyone's touch besides Ian, and Ella hadn't hesitated to make friends with the crippled animal.

And he'd been watching her face the whole time… there'd been no pity there. Just friendship.

So maybe he was a little confused, trying to second-guess himself, as he wrapped up the rest of her purchases. Manny sat on the opposite side of the counter with her, and she occasionally reached down to absentmindedly scratch behind the dog's ears. He'd never seen a woman do that with a dog as ugly as Manny.

"Manny doesn't usually let people touch him." He'd found the bloody and beaten dog tied near the DeVille ranch last summer, so it was understandable that Manny didn't trust anyone besides Ian himself, and that trust had taken months to build. "He's shy."

She was still smiling when she glanced down at the dog, but this time it was tinged with sadness. "Maybe I'm special."

Maybe she *was* special. But Ian didn't say anything more; just bundled up her wrapped purchases, took her money and handed back her change. It wasn't until she was walking out the door, those out-of-place boots clunking against the floor with each step, that he realized he wasn't going to see her again.

"Miss Ella?" She turned expectantly, and he lifted himself to his foot. "If you need anything else, I'd be happy to help you." He meant *if you need anything else to buy* but when her lips curled up again, he realized he'd help her with anything else she needed, too.

"Thank you, Mr. Crowne."

"Ian." He adjusted his glasses, more for something to do with his hands than a real need.

A slight nod, and those turquoise-blue eyes raked his shoulders and his forearms again. He watched her tongue dart out and swipe her upper lip, and knew that the sight was going to haunt him tonight. "Ian." His name was low and delicious on her lips, and he figured he wasn't going to get any sleep at all, imagining her saying his name over and over again.

And then she was gone, and Manny barked once. Ian sank down on his stool again, and dropped his hand to the dog's head to scratch. "You and me both, lad," he muttered.

Maybe she was special.

He didn't think of her again for the rest of the day; not while cross-checking his ledgers, not while waiting on his customers, and not even when he put the trimmings basket back under the fabric table. He didn't think of her while he fed the dogs some meat from the ice box in the back room, or when he gave them each a pat and locked up the store. He definitely didn't think of her during his quiet meal at Spratt's Eatery — the daily indulgence he allowed himself — or when he lifted himself up the back stairs behind his mercantile, using the double railing he'd had installed.

But after he pulled back the curtains of his lonely little apartment, allowing the slight breeze to cool the place; after he removed his vest and sank down to the single soft chair; after he felt Manny's head under his dangling fingers; *then* he let himself think of her. Think of her smile, of the way she'd been so patient. Think of her callused fingers and the how she'd looked at him admiringly, before she'd seen his leg. Think of *her*, and imagine what it would feel like to caress her dark hair the way she'd been caressing that velvet.

Ian sighed, wondering if the ache in his chest was bad enough to justify the trip over to the whiskey in the little kitchen. *Nah*. He'd learned ten years ago that using liquor to dull pain was a bad path to start down. Instead, he whistled, and Shiloh lifted her head from the mat in the corner. When Ian jerked his chin, the big dog bounded over happily, giving a deep rumble of contentment as Ian's fingers dug into the thick fur at the base of her neck.

Just him and his dogs. Like he was used to. Like he'd done every evening since Doc Bennett had told him that the fever had broken and it was time to go home to Philadelphia. *Home*. Home to a dead father and a mother struggling to maintain her share of the business. Home to learn how to walk with only one foot. Home to push himself to get out of bed every morning, to keep his parents' dream afloat.

Alone.

He'd always liked dogs, for their company and loyalty. When he'd found a giant hairy mutt freezing in the square that first winter home, he'd named him Culp, after the Hill where he'd lost his foot. After that came Getty, named for the larger battle. Shiloh and Vicksburg were next, and now little Manassas was the latest in his collection of strays and lost souls. They were his family, now.

With a groan, Ian hooked the ottoman with his foot, and propped his legs up on it. He peeled off his shoe—losing a foot meant he saved on shoes, at least—pushed up his trouser leg, and dug his fingers into the cramped muscle of his calf. Another groan, and Shiloh echoed it with a rumble. It felt *good*. Good to rest his leg, good to rub it.

His stump itched, but at least he didn't often feel the phantom pains from his missing foot that'd plagued him in the first few years after the War. It was his left leg that ached fiercely, most nights, from supporting all of his weight. He'd ordered the best crutch available—and with so many crippled veterans, there were plenty of them available—but he only used it outside of the store. In his little domain, his castle, he preferred to rely on his arm strength to navigate the counter, tables, railings and ropes carefully arranged so that he was never out of arms' reach of a surface to balance against. All of that, however, meant that his left leg did the work of two, and the muscle knotted accordingly.

And as he ran his palm over his calf, digging his toes into the cushion while he flexed the muscle, he wondered what it would feel like to have someone else do this for him. A woman. A wife. *Ella*.

His fingers stilled. Where had that thought come from? But now that it was in his head, he couldn't ignore it. Could imagine her bustling— she looked like the kind of woman who bustled— around the apartment, getting biscuits ready for tomorrow's breakfast, sitting beside him and discussing the day's business while sewing one of her dresses. Rubbing his leg until he groaned in pleasure.

The thought made his chest tight again, and he dropped his head back against the chair, ignoring Manny's whine of confusion. She wasn't here. No woman was, and no woman would be.

He knew that they looked at him admirably. Mother had been a beautiful woman, before responsibility and hard work had beaten her down, and Ian inherited her coloring. Oh yes; he'd seen the looks women sent his way, at church and on the street. But he'd also heard the things they whispered behind their hands. *Such a shame* and *If only* and *He'll never be able to*. And he had too much pride to court a woman who pitied him.

No, he wasn't getting married. Wasn't going to have a helpmate and companion and family. He'd gotten used to rubbing his own leg, and doing everything else for himself, and it was a good thing. Because he was going to remain alone.

CHAPTER THREE

Ella was in the vegetable garden when the screeching started. She exchanged looks with Maisie, and then bent back over her summer squash, returning to her private daydream of reliving every moment of that special day two weeks ago when she'd met Mr. Ian Crowne. Fights between Mabel and Eunice were common enough that she'd learned to ignore them, no matter if they were loud enough to be heard outside.

But this time, the screeching was getting closer and closer. Ella stood, pressing her hands against her lower back and *stretching,* glad for the big straw hat that protected her skin and eyes from the sun. Her toes flexed inside the old pair of cowboy boots she wore whenever she left the house, and Ella wondered if she could take them off and stand barefoot in the dirt like Maisie. It would be much more enjoyable, but she probably shouldn't risk it; the last time Sibyl caught her doing it, she'd tattled to Papa, who'd ranted about propriety and appearances and sent her to bed without supper.

Since she'd made the dinner, of course, the punishment was less effective than he might've thought.

Ella sighed. Her sister's complaint was still unintelligible, but it almost certainly had to do with something Ella had done, or hadn't done well enough. Mabel and Eunice's entire life seemed to revolve around coming up with more work for Ella. Sibyl was only fifteen, and had been such a sweet little girl when Ella met her twelve years ago... but her sisters were training her well, and she was becoming a snide and demanding young woman.

But it was Mabel who burst around the edge of the house, one arm full of pink silk. Her face was blotchy and her pale eyes sparked as she shook the dress on which Ella had worked so hard. "Look at this! Just look at this!" Her shriek could clean glass.

Ella, used to her stepsister's rages, just put her hands on her hips and waited for the complaints to start. Her calmness infuriated Mabel, as always. "Just what do you think you're doing with this thing?" She punctuated her diatribe by waving the dress around, and Ella considered moving closer, just so Mabel would stop screaming at her. But it probably wouldn't matter; she'd scream anyhow.

"What's wrong, Mabel?"

"You know good and well what's wrong! This doesn't look a *thing* like the fashion magazine! Did you follow the pattern at all? Where's all the *lace*? Where's all the..."

Apparently not able to handle the stress of her tantrum, Mabel sputtered to a stop. With an inarticulate scream, she turned on her heel and marched back towards the front porch. Ella winced, to see the beautiful silk dragging behind her in the dust.

When she heard the front door slam again, she turned back to the garden, and caught Maisie's disapproving frown. "Why do you let them girls talk to you like that? You ain't their slave, you're their *sister*."

Ella shrugged, and squatted back down in the dirt, pulling up the weeds that were threatening her careful rows. "Papa gave us a home. He let me stay here after Mama died." A death he probably caused, with the way he worked her so hard.

She heard Maisie's scoff, and secretly agreed. "Don't be acting like that was charity, girl. He didn't 'let you stay', he put you to work. You slave every day for that man and his spoiled girls."

"So do you."

"Yeah, but I get paid for it, now. No more slavery, Mr. Lincoln said. *You* don't get anything from your family 'cept more work and less appreciation."

Ella resisted the urge to swipe her forearm across her brow. Her hands were covered in dirt, and she'd just get messier... but *Lord* it was hot today. "I know, Maisie." Her admission was quiet. They'd had this discussion time and again. "But they need me."

A snort. "That's a load of trash, girl. They don't 'need' you, they just too cheap to pay someone to do the work you do for free. And until you stand up for yourself —"

"They're my *family*. I'm never going to find a better place." The lie sat heavy on her tongue.

Maisie didn't respond, and after a long moment, Ella glanced up to see her friend staring at her, a mixture of sadness and incredulity in her expression. Softly, so softly that Ella almost didn't hear, Maisie said, "You don't honestly believe that, do you?"

Ella swallowed, and tried for a grin. "No. But it's what I tell myself." She sighed, and tried not to think of the threats Papa had made over the years. "I've got to stay here, Maisie. I've got nowhere else."

She held Maisie's stare, willing her friend to believe that's why she stayed. Willed her to not glance over her shoulder, and see how every once in a while one of Papa's cowboys would stop his work and glance over, just checking to see that she was where she was supposed to be. Willed her to believe that Ella didn't lay awake at night, wondering if she should try to escape again, or if she'd be dragged back by her hair by Mr. Heyward, like that ill-fated attempt years ago.

"You could get married, move away." Maisie's suggestion surprised her.

"Married?" Ella snorted and turned away. "To who? Where would I find a man who'd marry me and take me away from all this?" She swept her arms wide, gesturing to the ranch lands that swept for miles in all directions, refusing to think of a pair of pale green eyes behind neat spectacles. "Papa made it clear that his daughters were off-limits to his workers, and Mabel doesn't let me join in on any of the teas or dinners she hosts." Although Ella made all the food for the events, and cleaned the house for them, and sewed the dresses her sisters wore to them. "And I can't go to town, because Papa is afraid I'll do just that—find a man and marry him and leave him and my sisters to fend for themselves." She sighed and propped her hands on her hips once more. "Maisie, I'm stuck here. There's not going to be a prince who'll ride up here in a golden coach and sweep me away. No princes know I'm here! Besides, I'm too old to believe in fairy tales. I've just got to make the best of things, and that means getting Mabel and Eunice married. We'll all be able to breathe easier then."

Her friend just frowned and shrugged, saying without words that she didn't agree, but there was nothing she could counter with. Ella's shoulders sagged as the tension eased, and she sighed. Every single thing she'd just said—not too politely, either—had been said before, often to herself. Ella had no other options, no way to leave. Papa had made it clear that she was going to spend her life here on the Miller Ranch, and made sure all of his men knew to keep her here. There'd been a few times, after Mama's death, when she'd attempted to go into town herself... the beatings Papa ordered Mr. Heyward to dole out as punishment had been enough to make her rethink escape.

Maisie's answer had always been to find a husband, and it was a good solution. Being married to some man—*any* man—would mean that she'd only have to cook and clean and slave for one person. No matter her friend's claims that it wasn't like that if you loved your husband, Ella had seen the truth of her mother's second marriage; chaining yourself to a man could be a living hell. But it was a hell she was willing to accept, if it meant getting away from this one.

Unfortunately, there was no way to. She hadn't been lying; Papa didn't let her meet eligible men, and she wasn't allowed to go into town to meet them on her own.

Except… except she had. Once. While her gaze roamed over the rolling hills and distant mountains, Ella was seeing Ian's easy smile and gentle way with the crippled dog. For the last two weeks he'd filled her thoughts, so much so that Eunice had noticed and taunted her. But Ella couldn't help it; he'd just been so… so *compelling*. She wanted to know all about him; how he ended up in Everland with his own store, and where he'd come from, and what he wanted in the future.

There'd been a horrifying moment, on the trip back from town two weeks before, when Ella had realized that she didn't even know if Ian was *married*. Maybe he was! Maybe his wife had been upstairs, tending their little ones and fixing a meal, while she'd been downstairs positively mooning over the gorgeous shopkeeper. But if he'd been married, would he have invited her to call him "Ian", and smiled the way he did at her?

Ella had convinced herself that it didn't matter; she was unlikely to ever see him again, and he could just remain in her imagination and her dreams. Because in her dreams, he was very definitely *not* married, and he'd ride out here to the Miller Ranch and carry her off someplace, and then kiss her. And *hoooooooboy* were the kisses nice ones. That first night, when his toe-curling, spine-tingling kiss had woken her from the most delicious dream, she'd laid there on her pallet, panting, and wondering where she'd gotten such an imagination.

Ian Crowne could *kiss*, even if it was only in her dreams.

Maybe she was distracted by the oh-so-real memory of his lips on hers, or maybe she just wasn't paying attention, but the next thing she realized, Eunice was standing at the edge of the garden, one hand on her hip and a smug look on her round face. "Daddy said that you have to come to his study right now."

And so, ten minutes later, a resigned Ella stood in her stepfather's study, staring at the bound books behind his desk that she didn't think had ever been read, but that she dusted every day, watching him listen to Mabel list her faults. They started with "lazy" and "incompetent", and Ella pretty much tuned them out after that. Mr. Heyward stood in his usual position behind her stepfather, practicing his glower and taking his job as his employer's enforcer seriously.

"So," Papa's deep rumble began, and Ella paid attention once more, "You're saying that your stepsister has done an inadequate job of following the pattern?"

Mabel was smirking when she nodded, and Ella managed not to show her irritation when she turned to her sister. "How have I not followed the pattern?"

Brandishing the fashion magazine in one hand and the pink dress in the other, Mabel gestured with both. "Look at this piece of trash. There isn't *nearly* enough lace on it!"

Ella *knew* that she should've locked the door to the sewing room—the only room in the house beside the kitchen that she felt any real ownership over—but then her sisters would've gotten even more suspicious. So she just tamped down on her sigh. "You told me, last month, that the sketch looked like—and I quote—'some kind of wedding cake with all those ridiculous frills'. So I cut the amount of lace in half."

"I would *never* say that. I *love* wedding cake!" It was true. Ella had been surprised at her sister's good taste at the time.

"I only bought enough lace to edge the three flounces, Mabel, because that's what we agreed to." Actually, she'd purchased enough for Sibyl's curtains too, but since those were complete, there was no need to confuse the issue.

Her stepsister gasped. "You're *lying*! You're lying to Daddy, to cover up your own incompetence. The picture has more lace, and I want *more lace*."

"Of course, baby. You want more lace, you can have more lace." As always, her stepfather's acquiesce to his spoiled daughter was enough to turn her stomach. But she hid her grimace when Edmund Miller turned his attention back to her. As always, he wasn't really *seeing* her, but his hard glare was certainly convincing. "I should've known that you would were too thoughtless for this responsibility, Ella. You really should have more care for your stepsister's needs."

Needs. *What about my needs*? But she'd long ago given up on mama's second husband being a real father to her, caring about what made her happy. So she swallowed, and hoped that her bland voice didn't betray her bitterness — having been slapped more than once for that fault — when she said "I'm sorry, Papa." The words twisted her stomach, but she forced herself to push through. "I can add more lace, with no problem."

Papa nodded, and she saw Mabel preen out of the corner of her eye. "Good. You can get started immediately."

"I don't have any more lace. I'm sorry." Apologizing, like it was her fault for only buying what they'd agreed to.

"Well, *go get some more*." Mabel's shrillness was very unattractive, but in that moment, Ella's heart lurched a bit. To get more lace, she'd have to go into Everland. And Pedlar Dry Goods was all out of lace; she'd purchased the last of it. But

Crowne's Mercantile... Ian had a bolt of lovely lace that matched this one very well.

So she kept her expression carefully bland, this time to disguise her fierce hope rather than her disgust, and cross to her sister. "Here," she said, her arms extended. "Let me see the dress. I'm sure I can find something to complement the lace."

"*More* lace."

"Sure, sure. More lace," she muttered, peering at the silk in her hands, much more concerned with how much damage Mabel had done by pulling it off the dressmaker's dummy and dragging it through the dirt than what type of lace she'd used. Luckily, the dress appeared okay. "I can go into town and get some more."

"Going into town?" Of course Papa wasn't going to like that, not with his successful campaign to keep her here on the ranch, and out of the townspeople's minds.

She plastered a vaguely admiring smile on her face and turned to face her stepfather. "I bought all of this exact type of lace, but I'm fairly certain that I saw a bolt that would match at one of the other stores." *Fairly certain*, as if she didn't remember every glorious moment of that trip into Crowne's Mercantile. *Fairly certain*, as if she was the only one capable of picking out the right lace.

He narrowed his eyes, and she held her breath, hoping that her stepfather would agree. After a long moment, he waved impatiently, and she knew that she'd won. "After breakfast tomorrow. Heyward—" His lackey smirked at the responsibility he knew was coming, " — will accompany you again."

"But, Daddy — "

Edmund interrupted his daughter's whine. "Tomorrow, Mabel. Ella can finish in the garden and work on your sisters' dresses before dinner today."

Oh joy, all in the next two hours? But Ella smiled. "Certainly, Papa. I'd be happy to."

And through the rest of the day — in the garden, adding the fringe to Eunice's green dress, fixing the chicken and cleaning up after — Ella knew that she was telling the truth. No matter if Ian Crowne was happily married, she was happy to be able to see him again. She just hoped that, when they met again, he wouldn't see the evidence of her deliciously naughty dreams on her face.

Because her dreams of Ian's kisses were the best part of her day.

Two weeks. It'd been two weeks since he'd seen her, and Ian couldn't get the sight of her out of his head. Worse, because of the incredibly realistic dreams he'd been having, he couldn't get the taste of her off his lips. It was galling, to know that he'd only met her once, exchanged a half-hour of pleasantries, and now dreamed of kissing her, of laying her back on his bed, and...

Embarrassingly, his dreams hadn't stopped there. He'd seen every inch of Ella — *felt* every inch of her — and he had his imagination to blame. He didn't know her family name, didn't know where she'd been from or where she'd been going, didn't know anything about her... but his sleeping mind didn't seem to care. More than once he's woken up, panting, on the verge of making her his own. And when he'd fall back on his pillow with a groan loud enough to wake the dogs, he didn't know if he was pleased or disappointed.

Two weeks of not enough sleep. Two weeks of Mr. Spratt at the eatery telling him that he looked sick, and getting uneasy looks at church. Maybe he *was* sick. Sick with desire for a woman long gone, for a dream he couldn't have. For a future.

Last night's dream had been so real that he was having trouble concentrating on his customers this morning. Just kept thinking of the way she'd beckoned him with that smile, and raked his chest with her gaze. Mr. Grimm kept having to repeat his questions, and finally joked about the shopkeeper's distraction. Ian took it in good humor, but was still glad when the older man gathered up his foodstuffs and left.

Breathing a little sigh of relief, Ian swung his way into the back room. It was cooler back here, without the windows, and more private. He told himself that he was going to check the supply of flour — Mr. Grimm had purchased more than usual — but suspected that it was just for a chance to clear his head. He was looking forward to lunchtime, when he could close down for an hour and come back here to sit and relax a bit. Maybe he'd nap.

A few deep breaths later, and he decided that his state of mind wasn't going away. He might as well close the shop now and take that nap, because he sure couldn't get his head on straight.

He pulled open the door again, grasped the railing he'd had installed, and was swinging himself out into the store when something caused him to look up. A change in the air? Some innate shopkeeper's sense that told him when a customer was around?

At that moment, it didn't matter. Because *she* was there.

She was standing in the middle of his store, a bag dangling from one shoulder. Ella was standing in his store, just like she had two weeks ago, looking at him like he was the most wonderful thing in the world. Not looking at his missing foot, or even his shoulders, but right at his face. At *him*.

Dear God, he'd gone and fallen asleep without realizing it. He was asleep, and this was another dream, although even more realistic than the others.

But then she shifted slightly, and her hand twitched in what may have been a wave, and her lips curved halfway up on one side. "Hi, Ian." She looked hesitant, unsure, and he knew that this wasn't a dream. His Dream-Ella never hesitated, but gave herself to him body and soul. No, this was the real Ella. She was really standing there in his shop, in her beat-up cowboy boots and the same blue dress from her last visit.

He knew, at that moment, that he couldn't let her walk out again. Not without knowing so much more about her, and why she was haunting his dreams. Maybe once he chatted with her, he'd be able to sleep better. Or at all.

Grabbing his crutch — he always kept it propped behind the counter in case he had to move quickly — he clumped past her, not caring that he was being rude. He had to make sure that she wasn't going to disappear on him again! When he reached the door, he used his crutch to push the rock holding it open out of the way, briefly wondering at the dangerous-looking man scowling at him from atop a horse outside his store. Dismissing the stranger, Ian took a deep breath and turned, afraid that she wouldn't be there.

She was. Her dark brows were drawn down over those lovely eyes, and a little frown marred her face. She seemed confused. "What are you…"

When she trailed off, he had to take a deep breath. She really *was* there. "I didn't want you to disappear on me again."

"Disappear?"

"After you left…" *I haven't stopped thinking about you.* This was ridiculous. He couldn't admit that. "I was sorry to see you go. I didn't think you'd be back." *I thought you'd be long gone.*

A one-sided shrug, and she looked down at her linked hands. "I needed more lace."

Oh. She needed more lace. That's why she'd come back? A part of Ian—a part that had been buried for over a decade, a part that had come back to life in the last two weeks—wilted. Of course she'd come back for more lace. He was a shopkeeper. He sold things that people needed. People didn't come here to see *him.*

"And…" She peaked up at him so fast that Ian would've missed it, had he not been staring at her face. "And I wanted to see you again."

Just like that, everything was all right again. A lightness filled his chest, and he felt like he could fly. She'd come to see him. *Him.* Ian's hand clenched around the crutch. Why did this woman and her reasoning matter so much to him?

She needed more lace. He hobbled towards the fabric table, hating the sound of the crutch on his shop floor, as always. "I think that the only lace I've got left is the stuff you looked at before."

"Good." He caught her smile as she gracefully navigated the maze of tables and counters and shelves, 'til she was by his side. And why did *that* thought make his heart beat faster? "That's exactly what I need."

He lifted up the basket, and when he poured out the trimmings, they both reached for the pile. And their hands touched.

It should've been nothing. A simple brush. It shouldn't have felt like liquid fire, running up his arm, as sharp and clear as the pain in his missing foot. It shouldn't have left him breathless and aroused and utterly incapable of speech.

But it did, and when he figured out how to move again, and turned to stare at her, she looked as shocked as he was. She cradled her hand in her opposite palm, as if she'd been burned as well. When their eyes met, Ian forgot to breathe.

He was leaning towards her, actually leaning in for a kiss, when she inhaled sharply, and the spell was broken. Ian reined in his desire and quickly turned back to the table. *No matter what you've been dreaming of, Ian lad, she doesn't want to kiss you. Doesn't want to kiss a cripple.*

It took a moment to find his voice. "So you didn't have enough lace after all?" Why did he sound like he'd swallowed his tongue?

She cleared her throat. "I guess not." Then a pause, and she took a deep breath. "No, actually, I did. I bought the perfect amount."

Confused, Ian picked up the bolt of lace in his free hand, and maneuvered his crutch to face her. She'd taken a step away from the table, but was frowning down at it with her hands on her hips now. "So, do you need…?"

God, she had the most adorable wrinkle between her brows when she frowned. Ian wondered if it appeared at other times, and if she'd be around long enough to find out. "Oh yes, I do need. Because it turns out that the perfect amount wasn't what I needed after all."

It fell into place. "Your client wants more lace?" It was a style choice that most shopkeepers approved of; the extravagant use of too much lace might make the wearer look ridiculous, but it meant more sales of the expensive trim.

Ella snorted slightly, and Lord help him, even that noise was enthralling. "You could say that. I *thought* she was being unusually frugal when she only wanted three of the flounces trimmed."

He couldn't help it; she was beautiful when she was perturbed. Ian smiled, and when she noticed, her frown deepened. "Are you laughing at me?"

His shrug was one-sided, as the crutch was still under his right arm. "I'm just glad that she wanted more, so that you had to come back."

This time she didn't blush and look away. This time, her frown eased, and her eyes cleared, and she stared at him. Openly, honestly. After a long moment, she confessed, "I am, too. I'm not usually allowed."

He filed that last statement away for future consideration. Who wouldn't allow her? "I've been thinking of you. Dreaming—" He almost bit his tongue, so fast did he clamp down on that confession. In his embarrassment at almost admitting his secret, he clumped past her—careful not to touch her again—and moved behind the counter.

But as he was putting his crutch back in its corner, and swinging himself towards his habitual spot on the tall stool, he swore that he heard her whisper "Me too." It was enough to make him close his eyes on an inarticulate prayer. *Please. Oh please.*

He focused on wrapping the lace, forgetting to ask her if she wanted all or just a length. *Shoot.* Glancing up to ask her, he found that she'd moved directly to the other side of the counter, and was smiling at him. Whatever he'd planned on saying ran right out of his mind.

"I'm glad that you still had that amount. With the July Fourth celebration coming up, I was terrified it'd be gone."

In the last week alone, he'd had six women come into his store, looking for ribbon for their gowns. That was four more than usual. Apparently, a ribbon-and-lace shortage was enough to make the ladies of Everland brave his presence. "Well, I sold about six feet of it a few days ago, but looks like there's plenty left." As if he had any idea how much lace a dress required.

"That'll be fine, thank you."

No. No, they couldn't be wrapping up their conversation as he wrapped up her purchase. He had to think of some way to keep her talking. "Truthfully, I assumed that you'd be long gone by now with your husband or family. The railroad is always bringing people in and out of Everland." Mr. Grimm mentioned that the group who'd been camped outside of town had also moved on, but that there were a few mysterious strangers still in town — like that man out front — and Ian had hoped that she might be one of them.

"Oh." *Keep talking, keep talking.* "Well, I'm not married…" Ian breathed a little sigh of relief. "And I didn't come by train." She looked down at her hands. "Actually, I rode my mule here."

She lived here in town? Everland had grown just in the three years since he'd been here, but Ian had never seen her before, not in church or out and about on the streets or at any of the admittedly few socials he'd attended. "I didn't realize that we had a seamstress here in town."

Ella's hands were flat against the counter in front of him, bracketing the now-paper-wrapped bundle. But judging from the tension in them, she was thinking about something besides her purchases. "I'm… I'm not a seamstress." She took a deep breath, and Ian pointedly did *not* glance at the way her breasts pushed against the thin blue cotton, afraid of what the sight would do to him. "I make dresses for my stepsisters. Papa believes that they should be very finely outfitted."

Only a fool could miss the bitterness in those words, and Ian was no fool. He took in her plain work dress, with the patches and the repairs made with small stitches. He thought of her work boots, and the calluses on her hands. Her father thought that her sisters should be well-dressed, and judging from the amount of money Ella had spent on decorations for their gowns, he was willing to provide. But for her? For Ella?

He remembered the sparks that had flown up his arm the last time they touched, but Ian could no more stop himself from touching her

than stop breathing. Without hesitation, he
engulfed one of her hands in his, and met her
eyes.

CHAPTER FOUR

Had she thought it shocking when Ian had accidentally brushed against her, earlier? When he took her hand in his, and turned it over to rub the pad of his thumb across her palm, Ella felt her knees give out. Thank the Lord she was already clutching the counter; it was the only thing that kept her upright.

His touch was sending alternating waves of shivers and heat up her arm and across her chest. She felt her nipples harden against her chemise, and thought that she might've died of shame if she wasn't already dying from sheer pleasure.

But then his thumb traced the calluses at the top of her palm — years of gripping a broom — and on the tips of her fingers — cooking burns, mostly — and reality came crashing back. No matter *how* deliciously good it felt to be touched by him, it wasn't right. He was a successful, respectable member of Everland society, and she… she was just Ella.

She'd already revealed too much about herself, and knew from the pitying look behind those spectacles that he'd figured out her secret shame. Her family was wealthy, but she was treated like a slave—he was touching the callused proof right now.

If he asked her anything else, if she *answered* any more of his questions, if he learned anything more about her… Ella knew that she'd start to dream the impossible. Dream of finally having a way to leave her family. Dream of Ian Crowne, offering to rescue her. Dream of marrying *him*.

If he knew what she was thinking—dreaming—he would've locked his door with her on the outside. But now… now, she just wanted to make him smile again.

Pulling her hand from his had the opposite effect, though. Good Heavens, he was handsome, with the faint freckles across the tops of his cheeks, even when he frowned. She wanted to smooth away the little lines at the edges of his eyes and the corners of his mouth, but couldn't.

Instead, she pulled down the large drawstring satchel she'd strung over one shoulder, and held it up. His lovely blue-green eyes followed it, questioningly. Suddenly, she felt shy, nervous about what she'd planned last night. "I brought lunch. Would you… share it with me?"

Rust-colored brows shot up in surprise. "You would do that? For me? Sharing your food?"

Ella shrugged, a little embarrassed that he was making such a fuss over it. He didn't need to know that she'd made extra fried chicken last night for just this purpose. "Of course. I have extra…"

Was it her imagination, or did his eyes soften a little? She could feel his gaze caressing her face—could feel it even with her eyes closed!—and she loved the delicious little shiver that ran down her back. Apparently the promise of food was the way to make him forget other concerns. And that would be important to remember, except that Ella wasn't sure if she'd be able to see him again after this. As it was, she wasn't sure how much time Mr. Heyward would give her before he got bored and came into the store looking for her.

"Yeah." One corner of his mouth quirked up, and he didn't look quite so serious anymore. "I'd like that a lot. Thanks."

She couldn't help but admire the play of muscles across his forearms as he grabbed the rope overhead and the shelving behind him, and heaved himself through the back door of the shop. It really was ingenious, the way he'd arranged the store so that he didn't need his crutch to get around; he could reach everything by balancing and supporting himself on the ropes, the rails, and the tables or shelves. Ian Crowne was an intelligent—and obviously very powerful—man.

She slipped around the counter and followed him to the back room, where she found him turning over a barrel for an extra seat, and calling stern instructions to his dogs, who tried to climb all over her.

Laughing, Ella fended them off, even though the largest was big enough to knock her over. "They're probably just smelling the fried chicken."

"You made fried chicken?" Was it her imagination, or did he sound as eager to eat as she'd been to spend time in his company? "Shiloh, get down. That's my chicken!"

The big hairy beast that had been lying on the front porch during her last visit was trying to plant his front paws on Ella's chest, but she managed to keep the satchel out of the reach of his jaws, laughing and pushing him away. Ian was laughing too, and had she thought his smile was nice? Goodness gracious; his laugh was pure *Heaven*!

He finally hoisted himself onto the barrel, calling the dog to him with a whistle. "Shiloh! Come here, boy!" He pulled down a bundle from one of the shelves, and unwrapped a full loaf of bread. She watched as he broke off a piece for himself, and then a tore the remainder in half. Shiloh sat on his haunches and watched the loaf eagerly, and she giggled when Ian made the poor thing wait patiently. Finally, after a stare-down — it was amazing how the big animal did what Ian wanted, even without commands! — he relented, and tossed the larger hunk of bread to the beast.

Ian seemed more relaxed back here than he'd been in his store, with her. "Sorry for his manners. He was hungry."

She'd sat in the only chair, and unpacked the food on the small table beside it. Fried chicken, cornbread and a miniature blueberry pie in a small tin were soon laid out, and she noticed that Ian was eying the meal hungrily as he apologized for his dog. She waved away his excuse. "The poor thing had to make do with bread when he could've had my chicken? No wonder he was fussing." She noticed that Ian smiled over her boast, and that Shiloh seemed content to chew on his bread.

Ian took the piece of cold chicken she passed to him, and shrugged sheepishly. "This is our usual lunch." With his free hand he opened the bundle beside him on the shelf, and Ella saw what looked like salt pork or bacon, and a shriveled apple. "Dogs know they don't get meat until dinner." He'd looked like he was going to say something else, until he bit into her chicken; and then he just hummed in what she hoped was pleasure. She watched his eyes sink shut behind those spectacles, and he chewed in silence. Taking a bite of her own piece, Ella enjoyed watching him.

Finally, he opened his eyes and pierced her with a serious look. "Miss Ella, I don't think I've ever had chicken this good."

She covered her discomfort with the compliment by taking another bite herself. A hasty chew-and-swallow, and he was still staring, so she tried a smile. "It's not that big a deal, Mr. Crowne."

"Ian, please." She thought that she might've nodded, but it was hard to say, with her chest so tight at the regard she saw in his expression. "And it *is* a big deal. We've never had company for lunch before, especially not such

pretty company. And the food is… well, it's a
welcome treat. Thank you."

Oh my. He had this way of staring at her
that left her… stared at. It was like his glasses
focused all of his intensity to one spot, which
entered through her soul and settled into her
stomach, where he made it hard to breathe. She
was embarrassed by his praise, but also secretly
thrilled by it.

And now he was waiting for her to say
something—*anything*—so she latched onto his last
statement. "'We'? You eat lunch with the dogs
every day?"

He chuckled. "I do almost everything with
the dogs. I'd end up eating dinner with them, if
Mr. Spratt didn't chase them out whenever they
try to follow me." Wasn't Spratt's the eatery she
heard Eunice speaking about last year? Most of
Ella's knowledge of the town came from
eavesdropping on her sisters' conversations about
their social engagements.

She handed him most of the cornbread,
loving the way that he enjoyed her cooking. It
was nice to see someone appreciating her hard
work… especially a *someone* as handsome as Ian.
"So this big guy here is Shiloh—" the large dog
lifted his head from where he was contentedly
gnawing on the hard loaf and gave a little *woof* at
hearing his name. "—and the little one is Manny."
Ian tossed the three-legged animal a bite of bread,
and it yipped excitedly. Ella tossed her chin at the
third animal. "Who is that?"

The last dog was medium-sized, with big floppy ears, short legs, and a belly that almost touched the ground. It was chewing on another hunk of bread, and when it lifted its head, Ella could see the long gray hairs around its muzzle and chin. "That's Vick. She's a good old dog, aren't you, girl?" The animal gave a half-hearted thump of her tail before going back to her meal, and Ian shrugged apologetically. "She doesn't hear so well anymore. Among other things."

Ella had to laugh at his exaggerated eye-roll. "So, Shiloh—" another bark, "Vick and Manny?"

"Vicksburg and Manassas."

"Ah." Northern victories in the War. "You were a soldier?"

"I was a quartermaster's assistant with the 28th Pennsylvania in the Twelfth Corps." He dropped his gaze to the chicken in his hands. "I thought that it would be a good way to use my skills."

"Were you a shopkeeper before the war?" Ella took another bite, but the food wasn't nearly as compelling as his history.

"Yeah. My parents owned half-interest in a store in Philadelphia. It was in my blood, and I figured I knew it inside and out." He took a bite, and said around it, "Quartermastering was more fun than soldiering, anyhow. But…" He swallowed, and she could tell it was more than just his food. "But I guess I had to pick up a rifle someday."

Unbidden, her gaze dropped to his missing foot, wondering what kind of horrors he'd seen during those battles. When she glanced up again, he was staring at her, and it wasn't a nice stare. He looked... bitter. Expectant. "After, I came home to try to learn how to do everything again, and I found that dogs were... helpful." He tossed a piece of meat to Manny, who snatched it out of mid-air. Ian's expression didn't change. "I named my first one Culp, and the next gal to make her way to me was Getty."

"Gettysburg." She'd read everything that she could on the battle where her real Papa had lost his life.

His chin jerked once, agreeing. "It was a rebel sharpshooter who did this to me." He thumped his right leg against the barrel he was sitting on, and Ella winced for him, although it didn't seem to hurt. "Either he had the worst aim, or was on his way down already, or something." Another bite, another moment of silence, another yip from Manny. "I felt the bones in my foot shatter. Actually felt them."

That's when he looked at her again, pinning her with his stare expectantly, like he wanted her to react. "Maybe they could've done something, had I been in Philadelphia. But out there, the best they could do was cut it off and hope I didn't bleed to death."

"I'm sorry." What else could she say? What else was he expecting her to say? "You must've had to be very strong, to survive that."

He looked almost…disappointed by her observation. When he shrugged, she saw the muscles rippling across his shoulders and down his bare arms at the movement, and thought about his rails and ropes and crutch. "I was never a small lad."

"No, I mean…" She wiped her hands on the napkin she'd wrapped the bread up in, not sure how to make him understand. "I mean, *you* were strong. Your will, your mind. Your heart. That sort of thing broke lesser men."

"I was seventeen." His whisper was so faint, she barely heard it, and had to look away so that he didn't see the tears that came to her eyes at that admission. So young, to have endured so much! To overcome so much!

She had to clear her throat before she trusted her voice. "But it didn't break you. You came out here, started your own store…?" She had to change the subject, or she'd break down, thinking of his pain.

"Not before losing everything in Philadelphia." He sighed then. "My father died while I was gone, and my mother had to deal with a crippled son and half of a store. I had to get better to help her. She lasted another five years before she gave up, and I sold the share I inherited and saved up to come out here. There's more opportunity out west, and I knew with all the settlers coming through, there was demand."

Ella passed him the pie. He took it without looking, watching her face. It wasn't until he glanced down to see what he held that his expression changed, softening to an easy grin. "Blueberry pie? How'd you know my favorite?"

"I guessed." She stifled her giggle, pleased that he was smiling again. "I am impressed with your strength, Mr. Crowne."

"Ian."

"You have a successful store, Ian, and you're living your dream." If only she could live some of her dreams… maybe even the ones that involved him?

At the word "dream," Ian looked up sharply, the fork halfway to his lips. "You think this is my dream?" He looked around the small, cool storage room, down at the dogs at his feet, and at the pie in his hand, and he shrugged. "Well…" He finally took the bite, and his eyes lit up. "A beautiful woman bringing me delicious foods might be part of my dream, after all."

The sight of his lips, carefully pulling the bite of pie from the fork, had nearly made Ella faint. She was leaning forward in her chair, only a heartbeat away from touching him. "What's the rest of your dream, Ian?"

He was staring at her while he chewed, and as before, she felt it right to her core. What was it about this man that made her want to touch him? To know all about him? To dream *with* him? While she watched, he slowly put the fork and the half-finished pie down on the shelf beside his usual lunch, and wiped his hands on his trousers.

Taking a deep breath, he watched her, as if struggling with a decision. His chest expanded, straining his gray vest until she thought the buttons might pop. Realized that she wouldn't mind it at all, if she got to see more of the skin that peaked out at his collar. He rubbed the back of his neck, and swallowed. "The rest of my dream would be to have a partner. Someone who could help me in the store, bring in more customers, since apparently lady customers don't like me on my own. Someone to talk things over with, and who'd give me an opinion, rather than just barking." His lips twitched when he glanced at Shiloh, but his eyes quickly found hers again. "Someone to make a future with."

"It sounds like you want a wife." The words were out before she could stop them, before she could tell herself not to be too forward, too desperate, too hopelessly attracted to him.

But he didn't smile. Instead, he nodded. "I'd never considered it, until recently. Until I—" *Met me?* But he didn't say it. He looked away. "I want a partner who sees *me*, not..." He knocked his stump against the barrel again, and trailed off, as if he didn't need to point out that he wasn't whole.

I see you, Ian Crowne.

But she didn't say it. Instead, they talked about his store, and his dogs, and his dreams. He asked her questions, and soon Ella's head was pounding from trying to come up with new ways to not answer them. She didn't want to talk about her life on the Miller Ranch; didn't want him to know how different it was from the freedom he enjoyed. Didn't want him to know that her

stepfather's man was waiting outside right now
for her.

Ian was strong, and committed, and kind
to animals, and to a girl like Ella, he was a prince.
She swallowed, ashamed of her sudden desire—
desire for *him*, but also for what he could offer
her. Was he looking for a wife? Would he ever,
possibly, consider someone like her? Someone
who could work hard, but didn't know much
beyond cleaning, sewing, cooking, and
housekeeping?

And was she being too presumptuous to
even consider the possibility? He was a successful
storekeeper who hadn't said a thing about her
more than appreciating she brought him food.
She was a silly girl who dreamed impossible
dreams.

"I have..." She swallowed down her
shame. "I have to go. To cook dinner."

"For your stepfather and sisters?" Why
did he sound angry? She nodded warily, unable
to think of a way to side-step the question. "Do
they pay you? Do they help you?" She jerked her
head again, but his voice—forceful and
compelling—stopped her. "Do they?"

She had no choice but to answer. "No,"
she whispered.

"You came here to buy them lace so that
you could make them a dress, and now you're
going home to cook for them? Will you clean
too?" His hands were fisted on his knees, and Ella
sank lower in her chair, knowing that she had to
answer him, but unable to make her voice work.

She nodded. "And what do you get from all of this? Their gratitude?"

"No."

"Then why do you do it?"

Because I have nowhere else to go! But she couldn't admit that, wouldn't. Not to him. He was a decent man, and he would pity her. She would rather he admire her, or at least, remember her fondly. She couldn't stand to know that he pitied her. So instead of answering, she began to gather up the remains of their lunch. There wasn't much; Ian had eaten most of the chicken and half of the small pie.

He watched her in silence, but when she stood to leave, he slid off the barrel, catching hold of her forearm. The heat that sparked from his touch stopped her, and Ella forced herself to swallow and meet his gaze. He stood a good six inches taller than her, but that didn't intimidate her. In fact, she felt safe, standing beside him; felt protected by his broad shoulders and his strong arms.

His hand ran down the length of her forearm, grasping her hand, and she shivered slightly. His expression was so serious, and not even the lock of rust-colored hair that had fallen over his brow distracted him. Instead, he squeezed her hand, and pinned her with the intensity of his gaze. "I'm sorry, Ella. I shouldn't have pushed you. I just… I wanted to know more about you." Oh dear, she'd forgotten how to breathe. "You are a woman I'd very much like to know more about."

Licking her lips, she tried to get a sound past them, but no luck. Instead, she just nodded quickly, hoping that she could draw a breath before she passed out.

He seemed to understand. "Thank you. Thank you for visiting me, and for sharing your lunch with me. It was the best meal I've had in a long while. The company ensured it."

Oh God. Now she had to add weak knees to her list of complaints. He was going to make her faint with his compliments and heated stare. Ella did the only thing she could; she pulled her hand from his and murmured "Thank you for the lace."

Then she turned and ran from the store.

CHAPTER FIVE

Thank you for the lace?

He had poured his heart out to her, there in his back room, and that's how she responded? "Thank you for the lace." Ian groaned aloud, putting down his fork long enough to rake his hand though his hair, not caring that he mussed it. It'd been three days since that beautiful hour spent in her company, and he'd done his best to stay busy. But here, sitting at dinner alone, his thoughts naturally turned to her, and all of the things he'd done wrong.

She'd come into his store to buy lace. *Lace.* That was it. She's shared her meal with him, probably out of pity and Christian charity. That was it. There was no need to read more into it.

Every time he thought of the way he'd touched her, held her hand, his stomach clenched in shame. He'd made a fool of himself, which is something that he'd always swore he wouldn't do. He'd held her there, trying to tell her how much his company meant to him… after pushing her and pushing her for information about her family.

At the time, it'd seemed like a good idea; he wanted to know where to find her, and the more he thought about the calluses on her hands, the angrier he'd gotten. And when he asked her — did her family appreciate her? — and she'd said no, with her voice soft and her head hanging in shame... that's when Ian felt the rage building. He very much wanted to know where she lived, just so he could go beat some sense into her stepfather. Didn't the man know how special Ella was? Didn't he appreciate all of her hard work for his family?

But the angrier Ian got, the more she withdrew from him, until he had to force himself to breathe normally or lose her altogether. So, when she was leaving, he stopped her and poured out his feelings.

And she'd thanked him for selling her the lace.

Ian groaned again. God, he really was an idiot. She'd probably been horrified when he told her how much her visit meant. She'd turned and run the moment he finished, and he couldn't blame her. He'd spent almost twelve years missing part of himself; he couldn't do half of the things men in Wyoming did on a daily basis... but for some reason, he'd thought that she might be different. She might see him for who he *was*, not for who he wasn't.

He dropped his forehead into his palms, rubbing at his eyes. His pulse pounded in his ears, making his head ache and his teeth clench. This was miserable, and it was his own fault.

"What is wrong with you? Why you no eat *Senora* Spratt's stew?"

Ian moved his hands just enough to see *Abuela* Zapato hobbling towards his table. She was a short, plump woman who wore her extremely-out-of-date bonnet everywhere, and carried her cane as much for swiping at errant boys as walking. She insisted on being called "Grandmother" not just because she ran the local orphanage, but because she treated everyone like her children. She was one of Ian's few regular female customers, and over the last year he'd come to not mind her motherly habit of thinking that she knew the best for everyone. Today, though, she pulled back the second chair at Ian's customary dinner table, and sat down without waiting for an invitation. "You are sick again, *hijo*? Mary, she tell me that you are sick before."

Ian tried for a smile, and sat up straighter. Ignoring muscles in his back that groaned in protest, he dropped his elbows from the table. He glanced at the plate of Mrs. Spratt's delicious beef stew and thick slice of bread, and swallowed his sigh. "It's tasty as always, Mrs. Zapato. I'm just not hungry today."

"*Yo no te creo*! I leave the children with Rojita and Hank, I come to *chismear* with Mary, *no*? But we no talk, because I see you here, sighing and pushing food around. I hear you moaning from across the room! I think 'There is a boy who needs Grandmother's advice!' You are sick at heart, *no*?"

Ian stared across the table at the woman who was always so solicitous when she came to his store, always so sensitive and caring. Would his father had been so perceptive of his feelings? Had his mother ever pushed him to share, like Mrs. Zapato was doing? "You're right. I'm not feeling well today."

"It is because of a woman." It wasn't a question.

"How did you...?"

The old woman shrugged dismissively. "When a man looks the way you look, *hijo*, it is because of a woman. Always."

Her expression invited him to spill everything, but Ian couldn't bring himself to share. Ella was... Ella was special, and secret, and only his. So he pressed his lips together and looked away.

Abuela Zapato sighed. "You are a lonely man, Ian. Your dogs, they not give you everything you need. You need conversation and connection and comfort. You deserve these things, Ian."

Do I?

"You need *esposa*. A wife."

He couldn't help himself; he snorted. A wife. He used to court women and steal kisses and make plans for futures together. But he'd had to forget those plans twelve years ago, lying on a table in a field hospital with a leather strap in his mouth for the pain and a blurry doctor standing over him. Mrs. Zapato's quiet words broke through the unpleasant memory. "You think you do not deserve these things? Deserve a wife? You are wrong."

She drew Ian's attention when she shifted forward in her seat, moving one veiny, callused hand to the tablecloth. "You are a good man, Ian Crowne. You have a business that is a success, you work hard. You have a home and a life to offer a woman. So you are missing a foot? *Pah!*" The old woman threw up her hands, but didn't let Ian drop her gaze. "That is not so very important. What is a foot? Nothing, to a husband, to a father." *A father?* It had been years since Ian had let himself dream of becoming a father. "You think your worth left with your foot? You are wrong."

Ian swallowed. Everything *Abuela* Zapato was saying… was true. He could recognize that; he was an intelligent man. So why was it so hard to make his heart accept this as truth?

Maybe the older woman saw something in his expression—some indication of how lost he felt—because she reached across the table and patted his shoulder. "You are a good man, Ian Crowne. You need to stop hiding, *no?* Stop hiding yourself and your heart."

"How?" God, his whisper sounded pitiful, but she only smiled, and squeezed his shoulder.

"Eat, first, or Mary will be mad. Then, join Everland. Make friends." Ian wanted to protest that he had friends, but at that moment, he couldn't name a single one. "Go to the saloon, go to your Sunday social—I know about this, I do. Meet people. Meet women. Meet your woman."

Mrs. Zapato patted him once more, and then stood and shuffled off towards the door. *Meet your woman.* Surely it wouldn't be that easy? Despite the fact that he rarely socialized, Ian knew most of the people in town, and hadn't heard of a woman who was forced to slave for her family. But if she hadn't left on the train, she *must* still be here somewhere.

Because no matter what old *Abuela* Zapato said, he didn't want any other woman; he wanted Ella. He wanted the woman who had looked at him and saw *him*.

But he *could* take Mrs. Zapato's advice. It would gain him… what? Acceptance. Because if nothing else, these two brief interactions with Ella — and the dreams he'd had in between — had taught him that he wanted more from life than what he had. Was *ready* for more from life. And gaining acceptance in Everland — showing them all that he was here and he wasn't going away, no matter what they thought of him — was the way to go about that.

And so, he ate the rest of the beef stew. And then, thanking Mr. Spratt with a smile, he collected his crutch and made his way towards the saloon. To make a place for himself in this community.

Mabel's dress was a monument to lacey gaudiness. All three pink flounces were lined in lace; there were thick lace borders at the wrists, neck, waist and shoulders; and thinner versions at absolutely every seam. It had required Ella to remove most of the stitches she'd already put in to add the lace, and the finished dress was… Well, she thought it was hideous, but Mabel was pleased.

"Ella, I have to admit that sometimes you aren't completely useless." Her oldest stepsister was standing on an ottoman, admiring herself in the sewing room's full-length mirror. Her twisting and turning was making it difficult for Ella to keep the hem she was pinning straight. If she could get this finished soon, maybe Mabel wouldn't insist on adding lace to *this* part too.

"You're too kind," she muttered around a mouthful of pins, rolling her eyes in the direction of her sister's shoes. "Now hold still."

Mabel tsked. "What do you think, Sibyl? Is there enough lace?"

Ella peeked at the girl sitting at the vanity and flipping through a magazine Papa had sent away for. Her pretty little lips curled up in distaste, but she lifted the pages so that her sister wouldn't see, and made a vague noise of agreement.

Hiding her own smile, Ella hurried through the pinning. In her opinion, this youngest Miller sister had the best taste in clothes, and wore them well. She was also the least-awful of Ella's stepsisters. Ella liked to think that it was because she'd helped raise the girl, and Sibyl had looked to her as a child as often as she'd looked to Mabel and Eunice. Of course, as she grew, and realized how much her family expected from Ella, she began to demand attention too.

But at least she only went along with her sisters; didn't think of the truly diabolical punishments as Mabel did. Why, on more than one occasion, Mabel waited until midnight to sneak downstairs and kick soot all over the parlor rug, in revenge for one of Ella's irritated retorts. Of course, she never admitted it, but her smug attitude — and the mess all along the hem of her nightgown, which she expected Ella to clean along with the parlor — was proof enough.

And Mabel found fault with almost everything that Ella did, no matter how well Ella did it. Just like this dress for the picnic; no matter that Ella had followed Mabel's pattern exactly, her older sister still found a way to make her re-do it. And Papa always, *always* sided with his daughters.

"The July Fourth celebration is only eight days away." Mabel was still preening when Ella looked up from where she squatted at her sister's feet. "I'm sure that this will be the year that I receive the proposal from the man of my dreams."

She'd said that last year, too, as Ella recalled. And the year before. But *this* year, Ella was in whole-hearted agreement with her oldest stepsister; Mabel *had* to get married soon. "Who is that?"

"Why, Roy DeVille, Jr. of course." The way she sighed his name caused one of Ella's brows to inch up on its own, and she exchanged a surprised glance with Sibyl, who'd dropped the magazine to listen.

"I didn't know that you…" How to put it delicately?" "Liked him."

Mabel put both her hands on her hips, still studying herself. "What you don't know could fill a rain barrel. His father owns the largest ranch in the area; it just makes sense that we'd marry and combine them. And he's so, so handsome…" She trailed off with another sigh.

Sibyl's mouth was pulled down in a little frown, but Ella wasn't sure why. She'd never met Roy—of course she hadn't—and so had no idea if he would be a good husband for Mabel. But then, what did it matter? *Any* husband would mean that Mabel was gone from her life.

"I don't think he's the kind to love you, though, Mabel."

Their oldest stepsister dismissed Sibyl's quiet claim with an eye-roll. "*Love*? Who cares about *love*? He's rich, darling; that's what matters. Only fools care about love."

Sibyl's chin came up, and Ella felt a little burst of pride at the girl's gumption. "I must be a fool, then. I'm only going to marry for love."

Remembering all of the novels and fairy tale books that Edmund Miller had purchased for his youngest daughter, Ella bent back over the hem. Sibyl had always been the romantic in the Miller family; she used to insist on Ella taking her

outside after the sun set to search for the first star
of the evening. She'd screw up her little face, and
whisper her wishing-chant to the heavens: *Star
light, star bright, first star I see tonight...* Ella hadn't
realized that the girl was still so ideological; she
wondered if this youngest stepsister of hers still
wished on stars.

"For love? In this town? Who would
possibly love you?"

Even Ella winced at Mabel's dismissive
insult. The Miller sisters were always chatting
about their social events and teas; surely there
were young men here who Sibyl could love? But
again, her youngest sister defended herself. "Any
number of them, I'm sure. Roy's brother Max is
handsome, in his own way. Or his friend Ox, who
seems sweet. Or Casey Jones, or the three Gruff
brothers, or even that handsome shopkeeper —
you know, the cripple."

Absolutely all of the blood in Ella's body
rushed to her ears to pound there, blocking out
Mabel's scowled response. She could tell from her
older stepsister's gestures that she didn't think
much of the town's offering of men. Ella's ears
began to clear just in time to hear her finish:
"...and as for Mr. Crowne, he's entirely too
reclusive. *Maybe* if he got out and joined the
community a bit more, *spent* some of that money
he must be hoarding, he'd be more attractive as a
husband." She ticked off his faults on her fingers,
blithely unaware of her angry stepsister, crouched
at her feet. "Maybe, *then*, you could consider
asking him to court you. *If* he could manage it —

how do you think he dances, with that crutch of his?" She dismissed him with a wave. "No, he's not real husband material."

Maybe not for you, you self-centered – Ella clamped down on her thoughts, afraid that they might appear on her face. Better to not respond to her sisters' discussion at all, than have them realize how badly she wanted to defend Ian. He was a good man, and didn't deserve to be insulted by Mabel. She willed Sibyl to defend her choices, but their overbearing sister must've beaten the girl back behind her magazine again.

Unfortunately, that meant that Mabel turned her attention back to Ella, who wasn't sure that she could speak yet, without betraying her outrage on Ian's behalf. "I hope that you've got our picnic baskets planned, Ella. I absolutely do *not* want a repeat of last year's fiasco." Last year, Ella had had the audacity to pack two baskets with the same food. "Eunice and I are doing you the favor of decorating our own baskets this year, so that you'll have time to cook." *Decorating? You're tying a ribbon around the handle, I'll bet.* Mabel smoothed her hair back, and pinched her cheeks slightly, still intent on her reflection. Ella resisted the urge to poke her with a pin and claim it was an accident. "The very least you can do is make sure that we're bringing different meals."

Ella *hmmmm*ed, not willing to agree, but knowing that it wouldn't make a lick of difference. Mabel didn't think that was the appropriate response. "*What?*"

"I said—" Ella moved the pins to one side of her mouth, her hands still working quickly. "That's fine. What does Eunice want in her basket?" Their middle sister was resting in her room with one of her frequent headaches, and the question was easier than asking what *Mabel* wanted, because she was sure to have a long list of demands.

"It doesn't matter what she wants, because you'll be making fried chicken for my basket. It's the least-terrible of the meals that you make, and would go well with potato salad, if you think that you can manage to make that without blundering completely."

The hateful words were easy to brush off. Everyone always enjoyed her fried chicken; Lord knows Ian had.

At the thought of Ian, her hands stilled. As always. She couldn't help but remember the intensity of his gaze when he'd held her hand there in his storeroom, and the way the heat had traveled up her arm and into her chest. He'd talked to her in a way that no man ever had. He treated her the way Maisie treated her; as a friend. And Ella loved every second of it. Loved seeing his smile, loved his teasing. She was still dreaming of him, but this time, her dreams were of more than just his kiss. Now that she *did* know what his touch did to her, she dreamed of grander things... a future together.

A sharp jab pulled her from her silly wool-gathering. Wincing, she carefully pulled the pin from her finger, careful not to get the drop of blood on the pink silk. A future with Ian? She had to scoff at her silliness. The man was handsome, successful, and well-off. She was a nobody.

"What are you doing with this, Ella?" Sibyl's question distracted Ella from her less-than-pleasant thoughts. Her younger stepsister was stroking a bolt of yellow-and-white cotton that Ella had been foolish enough to leave out. Her mouth went dry at the realization.

"Nothing," she managed to squeak out. Luckily, her work was hidden away at the back of the bottom drawer of the sewing bureau, where her sisters probably wouldn't think to look. Eunice had ordered the material last year, sight unseen, and when it arrived, Mabel had absolutely forbidden her to wear it. She said that with the Miller sisters' pale hair and skin, it made them all look like sallow corpses. Sibyl had obviously been disappointed, so Mabel relented and *allowed* Ella to make them all third-best summer nightgowns out of it.

There was still plenty of material left on the bolt, though, and Ella had thought that they might've forgotten about it. With the little bit of leftover lace from Mabel's gown, and a few feet of the leftover white ribbon from Eunice's gown, she'd thought that she could make a serviceable — but pretty — church dress… not that she was ever allowed to go to church with the family anymore.

Perhaps, in the very back of her mind, was the thought that — assuming her sisters' dresses were completed successfully, and that their food was packed — she might be able to go to the picnic too, if she had a dress fit for the occasion. Not nearly as fancy as her sisters'… but nice enough for Ian —

She bit her tongue, giving herself something to think about besides *him*.

Unfortunately, Mabel was able to sniff out secrets. "What do you mean, 'nothing'?" Her sharp tone sent a spike of pain through Ella's forehead, but she didn't let it show. "It's out, so it's obviously for *something*. What are you doing with it?" She tried to turn, to look at the fabric, but Ella held her ankle with her free hand, keeping her still so that she could finish the hem.

She pinned up the last few inches, frantically wracking her brain. *Curtains!* "I was thinking about using some of it to put up curtains in the kitchen." There was only the one window in there, and Ella definitely didn't need it covered — the more light in there, the better. But Mabel liked things to be pretty. "I thought it would go well with the dark colors in there." Now she was just making things up as she went, pretending to check that the hem was straight. "Maybe a few dish towels too? That way the room would be prettier, in case any of your guests wandered in."

She held her breath, waiting for her sister to take the bait. Her friends were as snobbish and self-centered as Mabel was, but she *did* occasionally host teas where she invited eligible bachelors, and the word "prettier" was a sure-fire way to get her approval. She liked things to be pretty, no matter the work that went into them.

"Well, fine then," Mabel *huff*ed, and turned back to preen at her reflection, and Ella gave a silent little sigh of relief. Her plans were safe. If she could finish up this hem before she had to start on supper, and if Mabel didn't think of anymore lace to add, then the dress would be complete. She still had a final fitting to do on Eunice's pale green silk... green the color of a pair of eyes behind spectacles — *Stop it!*

She shook her head slightly, trying to focus on her plans. She'd do Eunice's fitting tomorrow. Sibyl's blue dress was much simpler than her sisters', since she was younger, and could be finished a bit closer to the picnic with no one the wiser. That would give Ella a few hours each day — and maybe some at night, if she was willing to stay up and work in the kitchen — to piece together the sections of the yellow cotton she'd already cut. Even if there was no ribbon or lace left to trim with, she could always make a few small ruffles out of the scraps. And then, after the picnic was over, of course, she'd have to actually make curtains for the kitchen.

Assuming that Papa wasn't livid at her for daring to request to come along. Of course, since this was the year that Ella was absolutely set on getting Mabel and Eunice married off, she hoped that he'd have other, happier things on his mind.

"Ella, Papa wants to see you!" Eunice's sing-song gleeful call from the hallway, combined with the direction of Ella's thoughts a moment before, caused her heart to stop for one terrifying moment. But then she remembered to breathe again, knowing that her sister had no way of knowing what she'd been considering.

When Eunice breezed into the room, Mabel spun around on the ottoman, knocking Ella back on her heels. "What do you think, Eunice?"

To give her credit, the middle Miller sister wrinkled her nose when she took in the gaudy confection that was Mabel. "Isn't it rather… lacy?"

Mabel sighed dreamily, having stopped her spin in such a way that she could twist over her shoulder to see the dress's bustle. "I know. Isn't it wonderful?"

Ella could tell that Eunice was about to say something hurtful—Eunice wasn't as mean-spirited as Mabel, but just as blunt—and hurried to intervene. "Did Papa need me for something?"

The distraction worked. Eunice grinned spitefully when she turned. "Oh yes, Papa needs to see you right away in his study."

Glad that she'd just finished with Mabel's hem, Ella packed away the rest of her pins and placed the box on the vanity by Sibyl. Was it her imagination, or did her younger sister look a little pitying when she watched Ella leaving the room? On the way out the door, Ella called back, "Please leave the dress on the dummy, and I'll hem it when I get back." Mabel ignored her.

When she reached the door to Papa's study, Ella took a moment to roll her sleeves back down to her wrists, and straighten her apron. Papa was always very particular about her appearance, saying that there was no reason for her to look like she'd spent the morning in the ash heap... *even if that's where I was*. She also checked her reflection in the window in the hall, making sure that all of her little flyaway hairs were plastered down. Papa hated her hair—had hated Mama's hair too—saying that it made her look like a "gypsy devil." Since Ella had absolutely no idea what that meant, or what to do about it, she just kept her hair tied back tightly.

Straightening her shoulders, she knocked on the door. When his stern "Enter!" sounded from inside, she slipped through.

Papa's study fit him. It was sparse—his desk and two chairs, and nothing else—and imposing, with a wall of books that Ella snuck down to read sometimes. Mama used to read them to all of the girls, but when she'd died, Mabel and Eunice had quickly lost interest. Her stepfather was a big man, gruff and gray, who didn't want much to do with the same things that his daughters enjoyed. Still, he recognized that they were his heirs, and allowed them to have whatever they wanted.

"Good afternoon, Papa." He still hadn't acknowledged her, carefully perusing the *Cheyenne Leader* newspaper that she laid out for him every morning. Some days he was out on the range with the hands, working to support the cattle empire he'd built. Other days he was here in his study, working on his ledgers and correspondence, and giving orders to Mr. Heyward; those were the days that made Ella nervous. His inattention just made the pit in her stomach bigger.

Finally, he folded the paper carefully, and placing it on his desk, frowned in her direction. His stare wasn't pleasant, not like when Ian looked —

Ella hid her wince. *I'm not thinking about him right now. I'm not.* She couldn't afford to, not in front of Papa.

"Mabel showed me her dress yesterday." He folded his hands in front of him on the desk, and Ella blinked at the unexpected beginning. "It's... She seems quite pleased with it."

That was as close to a compliment as Papa was likely to give, so she smiled tightly. "Thank you."

His lips compressed in distaste, and she wondered if she'd gone too far. "I specifically asked her to show me what lace you added, after your second trip to town." Ella swallowed, the pit in her stomach suddenly wide enough for the mule to fall into. "It matches the other lace remarkably well."

He seemed to be waiting for an answer, but Ella had no idea what he expected, so she just said "Thank you" again, quieter.

"I find it interesting that you were able to go into town and find two such similar patterns." *Why? I spent a week working with that lace. I knew what it looked like.* "Where did you find it?"

She flicked a glance towards Mr. Heyward, hovering over Papa's shoulder, and was disconcerted to see that he was looking worried too. *Uh-oh*. "Pedlar's Dry Goods had the first bolt, but I'd purchased all of it. Crowne's Mercantile had the lace that I went back to get."

"Crowne's?"

"Yes, he had everything that I needed both times." Even as the words left her mouth, Ella winced, knowing that she was admitting more to her stepfather than she should. And that wince was even more telling. He'd know there was something she was hiding.

Sure enough, he leaned forward in his seat a bit, looking thoughtful. And a thoughtful-looking Papa meant that Ella was in for a punishment of some sort. She held her breath.

"Crowne's... Isn't that the Yankee cripple's store?" Ella cursed herself. She should've remembered her Papa's fierce southern loyalties. They were the reason that Maisie didn't work outside the kitchen.

Oh Lord, she'd gone and done it this time.

But despite Papa's anger—and she could see it simmering behind his eyes—she couldn't make herself agree with him. Couldn't relegate Ian to just a "cripple." It was people who saw him that way—people like Papa and her sisters, and people like himself—who kept him locked in the past, instead of looking towards his future. He'd named his dogs after the battle where he'd lost his leg, for goodness' sakes! If that wasn't living in the past, Ella didn't know *what* was!

But here and now, she just swallowed her words, and folded her hands in front of her dutifully, waiting for her stepfather to explode. When he did, he was colder than she'd expected.

"You have seen this cripple twice now, and didn't think to mention it?" He jerked his chin, and Mr. Heyward came around the desk to take the full brunt of Papa's glare. "You let her go into Crowne's *twice*?" Before his lackey could speak, Papa's anger swung back to Ella. "You were to go to Pedlar's Dry Goods—" Mr. Pedlar had come west from Georgia, and her father always shopped there—"not to some *Yankee's* store."

She had to keep her voice calm. "I know, Papa. But Mrs. Pedlar ran out, with the picnic coming up and all of Everland's ladies making new dresses. I had to go somewhere else. And like you said, Mr. Crowne's lace matched well enough."

Her soft tone did little to soothe him. Without warning, Papa slammed one fist down hard enough on his desk to make her jump. "You're defending him?" Ella swallowed again, and started to deny it, but he cut her off. "He is *nothing*. A nobody. I will not have any member of my household consorting with him."

It wasn't until she got light-headed that Ella realized she was holding her breath. And it wasn't until her stepfather sat back in his chair and stared at her contemplatively that Ella realized she was frightened. Papa had never raised his hand to her in anger, but he could be very inventive with his punishments. And she'd never transgressed quite this badly; she'd gone and fallen in love with a man.

Her knees went weak, and she had to grab the back of the leather chair to stay upright. *Fallen in love?* Don't be silly, how could she be in love? She'd only met Ian twice, only a few conversations with him. She didn't know a thing about him.

…Except that he was kind, and noble, and incredibly handsome, and polite, and… *Dear God, I* am *in love with him*.

She mentally scoffed. This wasn't one of Sibyl's fairy tales, where people fell in love at first sight. She couldn't possibly be in love with Ian Crowne.

But she was. And now Papa was looking at her like he'd guessed her dirty secret.

"I believe that I am the one at fault, Ella." Well. *That* was unexpected. "I have allowed you too much freedom, and like any senseless and rash young female, you've abused it." Freedom? The last thing she had too much of was freedom. "I've allowed you to go into town twice in the last month, which is two times too many. I allowed my daughters' foolish prattling about the perfection of their dresses to sway my long-held rule that you are confined to this ranch, and look what happened."

It was all she could do to keep her voice steady. His announcement, coming so soon after her realization, felt like it would crush her. "Mabel and Eunice's dresses need to be perfect."

"Yes, I am as anxious for them to marry as I'm sure you are. But that does not excuse your actions."

I went into town, like a normal person! I met a new friend, that's it! But Ella clamped her lips together firmly, afraid that if she said what was in her heart, Papa would find a way to make her punishment worse than what it surely already was.

"Heyward, you've been my right-hand-man for years, and I've trusted you." The man's habitual lewd smirk had been replaced by a vague look of terror, but Ella couldn't make herself pity him. "Because of that, I'll wait for my stepdaughter to leave before I issue your punishment." Heyward's face paled as the blood drained away, and his dread heightened Ella's.

"As for you…" Papa turned back to her, his eyes narrowed. "I should've known better than to think that you'd abide by the rules I set when your useless mother died. You will remain on my property. You will never, *ever* be allowed into town again." His words—his decree—sent a stab through her heart, and pressed a weight on her chest that crushed her. "Is that clear, girl?"

She couldn't answer, couldn't agree, couldn't say anything. He was planning to keep her here forever.

"What's more…" His evil tone drew her head up, her eyes seeking his pale ones glistening with malice. "If I *ever* hear your name linked with that cripple's again, I will *end him*. Do you understand?" No, no, she didn't. How could she?

She didn't understand half of what was happening. "I am a powerful man, and DeVille and I own most of this town. Ian Crowne could lose his shop, his home, and his livelihood, if we told people to stop shopping there." Papa leaned forward threateningly, but Ella didn't respond. She couldn't; she'd gone completely numb. "I can do that to him, and I will, if I ever hear his name in this house again. Do you understand?"

She might have nodded. There really wasn't any way to know. Her stepfather *would* do something that cruel, just because he could, because a man happened to support a different side in the last war, or because he wasn't good enough for the Miller name. But Ian was different, and so was Ella. What did it matter if the two of them…?

But there *wasn't* a "the two of them". Would never be "the two of them." Not now. Papa had made sure of that.

Two minutes ago, Ella had realized that she loved Ian. One minute ago, Papa had threatened everything he'd worked so hard to build, just because she'd met him. She couldn't love him, not now. Not when her loving him would ruin his life.

The ups and downs were too much; Ella thought that she might be sick. Maybe something showed on her face, despite years of practicing neutral expressions in front of her stepfather, because Papa just nodded, satisfied, and waved one hand dismissively. "Good. Go start on dinner."

She made it out of his study and down the hall and out the back door and halfway to the garden before she was sick. As she clutched her stomach in the hot Wyoming sun, tears streaming down her face, Ella prayed that no one would see her. She couldn't stand to see Maisie's pity or her stepsisters' smugness right now.

She'd lost Ian, before she ever really had him.

CHAPTER SIX

"Good to see you, Ian! How've you been?" Max DeVille slapped his back hard enough to spill Ian's lemonade, but it didn't matter. Ian just moved his foot away from the lemony puddle in the dirt and smiled, still a little amazed by the warm welcome the people of Everland had given him.

"Can't complain, Max. How about you?"

His new friend's usually energetic smile slipped just a bit when he shrugged, but Ian didn't think anyone else noticed. "Oh, you know how it is. Can find plenty to complain about, but it's too nice a day, so why bother?"

The two men shared a grin, and Max slipped into the open seat beside him. Ian had been chatting with three other men, but Gaston, Ox, and Hank welcomed Max enthusiastically. It was easy to welcome Max; the dark man had an open and affectionate personality that made everyone around him feel valued. Ian had felt himself falling under the other man's spell, but couldn't help it; it was hard not to smile and laugh around Max. He had a gift of making everyone's lives a little brighter.

The men continued their discussion about next week's parade and picnic, and Max chimed in. Ian, however, sat back and sipped his lemonade. *Abuela* Zapato had been right; he'd made an effort to get to know his neighbors, and suddenly he *was* a neighbor. He was accepted and acceptable and welcomed. He'd always attended church regularly, but had gone right back to the store to stock the shelves on Sunday afternoons. For the last two weeks, though, he'd stayed after the service for the weekly social with the cakes and lemonade, and had been amazed at the difference it made.

Suddenly, men that he'd known for three years—like Max—as just faces in the crowd were becoming *friends*. He'd visited the saloon another few times, and Max had introduced him to Ox Bunyan and a few others who welcomed him into their twice-weekly poker game. It was still a new sensation to Ian, to not feel like he had to hide himself… but it was nice.

Very nice.

Even now, they pulled him into the conversation about the basket bidding. He hadn't bothered to attend the last two years' celebrations, telling himself that he needed to man the store, just in case. So he was enjoying hearing all about the town's traditions. "So the gals, see? They pack a lunch in their basket, right? And you bid on 'em, the baskets I mean, 'cause you want the gal or the food she's got in there, whichever." Ian kept a carefully neutral face, but could see Max laughing silently behind the earnest Ox. "An' sometimes her food *is* better, right? I mean, the rest of us are eating whatever is spread out—all sorts o' dishes and treats an' they're roasting two whole pigs this year—and it's real good. But when there's that special gal who's caught your eye, then her picnic basket don't matter atall, you jest gotta have it so you're eatin' with her, you know?"

Ox's earnest explanation made Ian smile. "I think I do." He was remembering a lunch shared with a "special gal" who'd "caught his eye", and that fried chicken had been the best thing he could remember tasting. But it was hard to imagine that Ella would be at the picnic with her basket. In the two weeks that he'd been asking around among his newfound friends, no one knew of a coal-haired beauty who sewed for her sisters.

"Well, I'm out. I've got all the woman I could possibly want." Hank Cutter stood and dusted off the denim of his trousers, while looking around for his petite wife. Ian found her chasing after four of her grandmother's youngest orphans, and jerked his chin in her direction, smiling at the way his usually stoic friend's eyes lit up at the sight. "And I'd better go help her, if I want to have any chance alone with her."

There was a bunch of laughter at that, and then a round of hand-shakes, and Hank ambled off towards the shrieking children and his exasperated wife.

The rest of them returned to the topic of the picnic. "You are planning on bidding on a basket, yes?" Gaston's accent was negligible after so many years in the country, but his sentence structure was still very Gallic. "There are many new women in Everland this year. They have come in by train for the celebration, and I have heard, maybe, of a *bel étranger* I would not mind meeting." Ian's attention was caught at the mention of a "beautiful stranger", but Gaston's next words dashed his hopes. "She has hair redder than Hank's *amour,* and purple eyes, apparently, but dresses as an old woman does, and drives a stagecoach." The Frenchman began to laugh, and when he jabbed Ox with an elbow and their friend scowled in return, Ian knew that there was more to the story. "Apparently, our friend here has seen this imaginary — I mean, *mysterious* woman."

Ian couldn't help chuckle when Max's guffaws started. "Yeah, but it was after a poker game, and Ox'd helped finish a bottle of whiskey, as I recall."

"Yes." Gaston tried for a serious nod. "So maybe it is not likely she will appear for the auction, yes?" He turned to Ian. "Just as well. You should wish to bid on a real woman."

Ian shook his head slightly, but kept his grin in place. "Not this time around, I think. There's no one in particular who's caught my eye." Since they were still in the church yard, he felt a little guilty at uttering that lie, but tamped down on the urge and told himself it was true. Ella wasn't going to be one of the gals up there on that stage, waiting for a bid. She'd be the one who would tempt him; he'd pour all of last month's profits into making sure she shared her basket with him.

"No one who's caught your eye?" Max's good-natured grin was teasing. "Are you blind, even with those glasses?" He slapped Ian on the back again, and Gaston joined in his laughter. When was the last time he'd been teased by a friend? Ian couldn't remember. Probably in the army.

So he was grinning when he shrugged off the insult. "No, I just figured that I'd sit this year out, to give you another chance to bid on whatever young woman interests you. If *I* were bidding, you wouldn't stand a chance."

"What makes you so sure?"

"Well, I make a living knowing what people like. I'm refined, and well-dressed, whereas you…"

Max narrowed his eyes. "Are you insulting me?"

"I'm sorry, was I too subtle?" Ian's grin grew. "*You're ugly.*"

Ox's uproarious laughter was infectious, and soon all four of them were chuckling and slapping their knees and tossing insults. Max's dark complexion might've bordered on "swarthy" when compared to his golden brother, Roy Jr., but Ian had seen the way the town ladies eyed his new friend, and knew that he was considered a catch. Gaston had just pointed that out—probably to tease him—when Max turned their attention once more.

"I'm not the only catch! Do you see the way they're staring?" He jerked his chin subtly to the group of well-dressed young ladies standing on the other side of the yard. The five of them were spinning parasols and twittering at each other behind their fans, but Ian could see them staring, as Max said.

Poor Ox was nervous, not wanting to turn around and be caught staring back. "Are they really starin' at us? Which ones?"

"Rose and her sister Snow, and the Miller girls."

Ox's sigh was part satisfied, part dreamy. It would've been funny, if Ian hadn't sighed just like that a few times over the last month while thinking about Ella. "Them White gals is somethin' else."

"Indeed." Max jabbed Ian in the ribs. "But I hate to tell you; I'm pretty sure they're staring at our friend Ian here."

"Me?" It must've sounded like a squeak to his friends too, because they all began to laugh again.

"Yes, Ian." Gaston's huge mustache made him look like he was still laughing. "You are a catch, I have heard."

"*Me?*"

Ox was scowling. "He's not so great. Rose and Snow wouldn't want him."

The other man's words sent a shot of reality through Ian's good humor. "Because I'm a cripple."

"Nah, because you're a red-head."

Well, *that* was ridiculous. Ian's mood lifted as suddenly as it had soured. "What does that have to do with anything?"

Max leaned a little closer so that he could lower his voice, and gestured with his chin. "See the three blondes? They're the Miller sisters. Their father owns the second-biggest ranch in the area, behind my pa. The two on the left, though…" Ian sucked in a breath when the red-head turned his way. She was *gorgeous*. "Yeah. That's Rose, and her sister is Snow. I thought that might've been who you meant, when you were looking for your mysterious black-haired beauty. But Snow, bless her heart, can't sew worth a damn. And they're determined to have lots of golden-haired little babies, so that means you and me are out." He smiled again. "Ox still has a chance, though."

"And I aim to use it this year, long as you pretty boys don't get in my way!"

Ian chuckled and held up his hand, palm out. "I won't stand in your way, my friend." Rose was lovelier than Ox deserved, but there was no accounting for taste. "Why such an odd requirement?"

Gaston shrugged. "A curse, I once heard. Who can say, what a woman is thinking, yes?"

That earned another round of laughter and agreement, Max loudest of all. It… it felt good. Ian had no reason to be sitting here, laughing about women… but it felt *right*. Like he belonged.

"So Miss Rose is looking at Ox, here. Not me."

Max waved off his objection. "They're all staring at you, Ian. They *know* Ox. Look at Zelle standing over there with her father, Doc Carpenter; I'm glad he's let her out for this, she needs the chance to let her hair down every once in a while. Or Arabella Mayor, she's supposed to be watching her littlest play with Mrs. Boone's twins. They're all staring pretty hard." Moving only his eyes, Ian flicked his eyes around the church yard, noticing all of the eligible young women looking his way.

"You're the mystery man, Ian. The one who's been hiding in his shop. Yes you have," Max said when he started to protest. "You've got your own business, your own house. Not one of us cowboys, bunking with a bunch of smelly animals." He nodded at Ox, who scowled good-naturedly. "Trust me, I know women. Hell, I'm friends with Snow — since I'm off-limits as a potential husband — and even Arabella. Women want a man who'll keep 'em here in town, so that they can parade around to all their social events." Was it Ian's imagination, or was there just a hint of bitterness in his friend's voice?

He decided not to push it, but thought about Max's words instead of his tone. After years of hearing women's pity, it was hard to accept that he might have something to recommend him. But sure enough, the five lovely ladies across the yard, as well as others, had been smiling in his direction since he sat down here. Could Max be right?

But why would they be interested in him? They didn't know him; didn't know anything about him.

It wasn't until Gaston chuckled that Ian realized he'd said that last part out loud… and worse, had sounded like a whiny child in the process. "You wish to know plenty about them, I think though, yes?"

No. None of them had thick, coal-black hair and a skittish smile and a heart big enough to see *him*. But if he was going to make an effort to fit in here in Everland, he really should be polite. "All right. Tell me about them."

"Better yet, I'll introduce you!" Max slapped him yet again on the shoulder, and jumped to his feet, offering his hand to Ian. Without thinking, Ian let his new friend pull him upright, and didn't object when Max handed him his crutch. It hadn't felt pitying, it hadn't felt shameful. It was just a simple gesture of friendship, and Ian doubted that Max knew how much it had meant.

When they were both standing, Max smiled. They were of a height, but the other man's shoulders weren't as broad. "Sibyl Miller is too young for you, and Mabel Miller is too horrible, and Gaston already has a claim on Eunice." Ian heard the Frenchman mutter darkly. "And their father is a dyed-in-the-wool Confederate, so he wouldn't have you anyhow. The White girls, though…"

His new friend walked slowly enough that Ian had no problem hobbling along beside him.

Despite his gait—or lack of it—he hadn't felt this *equal* to another young man in… well, probably since this day, twelve years before. It was an odd feeling. It was a good feeling.

It looked like, thanks to *Abuela* Zapato's advice, Ian was going to be able to make a place for himself here in Everland, after all.

Ella called it "the magic hour"; that brief amount of time in the early afternoon between cleaning up from lunch and getting ready for supper. She tried her hardest to get her daily chores done in the morning, and as much of the cleaning as she could squeeze in. Usually, after making up her stepsister's beds and readying their wardrobes for the following day, she had to dust at least one of the downstairs rooms, and tidy the parlor behind her stepsisters. But then, right around two o'clock, she had an hour or so to focus on one of her own projects. Usually that was some sort of sewing.

She loved to sew. It had been something that Mama had taught her, all those years ago, to give her something to do to help support them. Some of her fondest childhood memories had been spent by Mama's side next to the warm hearth, bent over her tiny stitches and listening to Mama sing. Once they'd come out here to

Wyoming, Mama had still sewed, only then it was for four little girls instead of clients. Ella helped her, and when she died, the little girl took over her mother's duties.

The house was suspiciously quiet as she climbed the big stairs. She hadn't been aware of any social events this close to the big July Fourth celebration, but perhaps her sisters had found someplace to take themselves off to. Or they were ensconced in their own rooms, napping from the strenuous morning activity of giving her their demands for their picnic baskets. Mabel and Eunice insisted on everything being fresh, so Ella hadn't been able to get started on cooking yet. Tomorrow — the third of July — was going to be brutal.

For now, though, she had just enough time to put the finishing touches on her yellow dress. She'd finished Eunice's dress right after Mabel's, even though she'd been so horribly distracted by Papa's ultimatum. Hopefully, her sisters hadn't noticed, and Eunice had been as pleased with her fringed green silk gown as Mabel had been with her pink lacy one. Since Sibyl's had been finished as well, Ella felt okay staying up late to work on her own. It was... odd, to be spending so much time on a new dress for herself, rather than just fixing up ripped hand-me-downs. For the last few nights, she'd had to pin herself together, and then transfer the whole thing to her mother's wickerwork dummy to finish. It had been awkward and exhausting and wonderful. She'd never had a dress as lovely as this one, with its crisp white ribbon and the bits of lace at the wrist and waist.

Of course, thanks to Papa's new ruling, she had no place to wear it. She'd hoped to be able to ask — beg even — to attend the picnic, now that she'd have a gown worthy of being seen in. Papa and her sisters had always called her "dark and ugly" and didn't want her associated with them. At least, that was the reason Mabel always gave her for why she wasn't allowed to attend church or any of the other social occasions. But now, now she that she had a lovely new dress, Ella had been hopeful that she'd be allowed to come along too, even just to sit by the refreshments table and watch.

But her stepfather's harsh voice had put an end to that dream as well. *You will remain on my property. You will never, ever be allowed into town again.* Ella's heart clenched at the memory, and she sagged against the wall for a moment, afraid that the despair she'd felt when he'd uttered those words would never leave her. She was trapped here... forever. It almost seemed silly, to keep working on the yellow dress, as if she was ever going to be able to wear it anywhere. But it was the only thing that kept her smiling. She labored over the tiny stitches, and imagined what Ian would say if he could see her in it... And despite knowing that there was no future for the two of them, she couldn't force herself to stop dreaming about him. The many kisses that he'd given her in her dreams — the way that he held her like he would never let her go — were just that; dreams.

But they were her only bright spot in the last
week of disappointment, and so she let herself
relive them while she worked on the dress.

And today, Ella had an hour to work on
the final touches. It was probably silly to be
spending time on this project, especially when
tomorrow was going to be so busy, but she *needed*
this. She needed an hour to just be *Ella*, to work
on something to make *her* happy for a change.

But when she pushed open the door to the
sewing room, she found her sisters. Sibyl was
sitting at the vanity again, and Eunice was on the
ottoman they used as a stool, and Mabel was
standing the middle of the room. They all froze
when Ella entered, but it didn't matter. It was
obvious what they were doing.

All around them, spread all over the room,
were parts of her yellow dress. The dress that had
been almost finished. The dress that was going to
be her one new dress. The dress that she'd hoped
would be lovely enough to be allowed to be seen
in public with them. Without thinking, she took
two steps into the room, and then her knees
buckled and she sank to the ground, pulling part
of the skirt towards her and looking up
incredulously at her stepsisters.

Why would you do this? She wanted to
scream it, but she couldn't seem to make her voice
work; couldn't even make her breath work. She
watched Sibyl drop the piece of yellow cotton
she'd been holding, and place the tiny seam-
picking knife back on the vanity, a vaguely ill
look on her face. But Eunice and Mabel just

smirked cruelly. Ella's oldest stepsister lifted what remained of the dress's bodice, and yanked. With a thoroughly depressing *riiiiiiiiiiip,* the two pieces came apart, and Mabel smiled, satisfied.

It wasn't until her knuckle popped that Ella realized she was clutching the material in her fists tight enough to ache, but she couldn't seem to make herself stop. *Why? Why would you do this to me?*

Mabel's smirk told her that she understood Ella unspoken plea. With a flourish, she dropped the pieces of the lovely dress to the floor, and tossed her head dismissively. "You were using *my* lace, Ella dear, without permission."

You weren't using it. Ella wanted to defend herself, to explain that Mabel's dress had eighteen times the amount of lace — Ella would know, after all — and that since it was complete, Ella assumed that she could use the last few feet. But she also knew that any attempt to rebut Mabel's cruel words would result in a greater punishment. And besides, Ella couldn't seem to make herself speak. Her breaths were coming in short gasps, and she felt herself getting light-headed.

"Besides, I've decided that I want a bit more lace around the collar on my dress. So I needed to remove it from your dress, so you can put it on mine."

"You ripped the whole thing apart." It was part accusation, part incredulous question.

Mabel shrugged, as if her actions had no real consequences. As if Ella wasn't fighting the urge to leap at her fingernails bared. "Well, I was just going to take apart the seams with the lace—" Ella could read the lie in those cold blue eyes, "—but then I saw how poorly made the stitches were—" Another lie! "—and I called in the girls to help me."

Mabel took two steps towards Eunice, and scooped up the sad little pile of lace that had been on her sister's lap. Dangling it between her thumb and forefinger, so that it twisted and snaked with each movement, Mabel crossed to stand over Ella.

Ella refused to look up, to give her sister the satisfaction of craning her neck. Instead, she stared resolutely at the tail end of the lace, dangling in front of her eyes. But she could hear the satisfied smile in Mabel's voice when she said, "I'll expect this piece on my collar by this evening, Ella dear."

When Mabel dropped the lace into her lap, Ella couldn't make herself let go of the yellow cotton—what had once been her dress, her hope of *some* kind of excitement and pleasure—to pick it up. Wasn't sure if she could, without feeling sick from her sisters' casual cruelty.

Mabel swept past her, knocking Ella to one side, and Eunice followed, her chin up. Sibyl stood to follow her sisters, and made it as far as the doorway. When she paused, Ella forced herself to meet her youngest stepsister's guilty gaze. "For what it's worth, I think it was a lovely dress." Her whisper didn't linger any longer than Sibyl did, and then Ella was alone.

Alone with the remains of her dream.

CHAPTER SEVEN

July third was as hard as Ella had thought it'd be. Her morning was full of last-minute demands from her stepsisters, and her afternoon was spent in the kitchen. She had so much to do that she barely had the time to mourn her dress, and the lost chance it represented. Eunice's pasta salad was cooling, and Ella was plucking the chickens when Maisie came in to start preparing supper for the men. Ella was planning on serving fried chicken tonight, and prepping an extra half to fry tomorrow morning for Mabel's basket. Eunice's ham just needed to be sliced, and her cinnamon apples were ready to go. She still had to figure out cookies for both baskets, but figured that she could do that tomorrow morning.

Ella was so caught up in her menu — mentally listing everything that she still needed to do — that she just didn't notice Maisie's quiet mood. Usually the other woman kept her talking and laughing throughout the afternoon, but not today. It wasn't until Ella had gone out to wash the chicken feathers from her hands and forearms that she realized her friend's mood.

"What's wrong, Maisie?" Sometimes direct questions worked better than trying to guess.

Maisie shrugged, and continued to knead the dough for the night's biscuits. She was going to make a few loaves of her cornbread too; half each for the baskets, and the rest to take to the picnic to share. But her preoccupation had nothing to do with her cooking, Ella could tell.

"You know, if you just told me, maybe we could figure out a way to solve this." It was, word-for-word, what her friend had said to her yesterday, when Ella had returned to the kitchen, heartbroken, and clutching the remains of the yellow dress. She'd told the story in fits and starts, and soon Maisie was crying alongside her.

The other woman's lips quirked, and Ella knew that she remembered. They were friends, and friends told each other everything. So Maisie sighed, and punched the dough a little harder than was necessary. "Them DeVille boys be over here again. Guess they figure to start celebratin' early."

Ella frowned as she began mixing the ingredients for the chicken's batter. The Miller Ranch was the second-largest in the area, bordering Roy DeVille's spread on one corner. She didn't know much about the DeVille family, but some of the rowdier hands sometimes teamed up with some of Papa's hands for some devilry. It rarely spread to their home, but Ella could remember one summer where a wild group had ridden around, shooting and hollering like a pack of savages. It had been scary, even to a little girl who'd expected the worst from men.

"What nonsense are they up to now?"

"Dog-fightin'." Maisie's tight answer caused Ella's head to whip around, and her friend nodded. "Turns out they all been plannin' it for a while. I went out there to see my man for lunch, and a big group o' them is gathered behind the biggest barn." Her lips were tight, her movements controlled, and Ella knew that her friend was angry. "They baitin' and teasin' them dogs, 'til they angry enough to kill, and makin' them run after each other. Sometime one-on-one, and sometimes all at once. They all drinkin' and bettin' and hollerin' like it's a holiday already."

"That sounds horrible." She was being truthful; it sounded worse than their normal mischief. She'd known her Papa's hands to bet on fights or races, but pitting innocent dogs against one another? That was just plain cruel. Then she remembered the little dog in Ian's store, Manny; he was missing a leg and was awfully skittish, and she had to wonder what happened to him. Had he been in an accident, or had something more sinister happened to the cute little animal? Despite the heat of the kitchen, a shiver travelled down Ella's spine. Was this common? Did men often force dogs to fight for their entertainment, for sport? What happened to the losers? And where did they get the dogs to fight in the first place?

"Maisie, what dogs…?" She swallowed down the lump in her throat, suddenly not wanting to know the answer.

And it looked like her friend didn't want to tell her the answer, judging by the stiffening of her shoulders, which made Ella dread it even more. "Maisie?" she whispered her plea, and watched the other woman let out a sigh.

"You know the puppy we been raisin'?" *Oh no. Oh please, no!* "They got their dogs, their working dogs. Leonard says that they been trainin' them to fight and whatnot, but the pup…" She trailed off, and Ella braced her hands against the table, not caring if she trailed cornmeal and egg everywhere. This, after yesterday's disaster? Human beings could be *horrible*!

"They're using her to fight other dogs?" A few months before, one of the ranch dogs had whelped, and then disappeared. This pup was the last one left, and Leonard and Maisie had been taking care of her. Ella loved to go out and visit the little thing; she was still at that gangly puppy phase where her feet were too big for her body and she kept tripping on her ears. She was positively the most adorable thing Ella could imagine coming out of the Miller Ranch, and it made her ill to think that people could waste that so casually.

"Is she dead?" It hurt to ask, but she had to know. The dog was just a dog, but coming right on the heels of yesterday, this news just made her more upset at her family and the men they employed.

Maisie began to work the dough again, her sharp movements telling Ella that it wasn't a good story. "The dog ain't dead, but not for lack of tryin'. Leonard says she gunna be soon, anyhow. Her side is all tore up, and she breathin' hard."

Ella let out the breath she'd been holding, when she heard Maisie's response. Of course. Of course the dog would die, and there wasn't anything she could do about it. And she wasn't even sure if she could care; it was just a dog. Just a dog who'd had a rough start in life, but who was finally ready to take on the world. Just a dog who had made Ella smile a few times, when she didn't have any other reason to smile.

Just a dog like Manny. Like Shiloh and Vicksburg and the other dogs Ian had loved.

Ian had loved.

Suddenly, Ella couldn't stand the thought of the pup dying. She felt her gut clench and her chest tighten, and she knew — *knew* — that this wasn't "just a dog". This was a dog that had been abused and ruined by people who were supposed to be taking care of it. This was a dog that had been hurt by her family.

Just like she'd been.

She couldn't go take back all the times she'd given in to her sisters over the years, or all the times she'd taken her stepfather's punishments because she had no other alternative, no other home. She couldn't erase the hurt and the pain that she'd endured for over a decade… but maybe, just maybe, she could make up for it. The pup hadn't done any more to deserve her pain than Ella had, but she was strong enough to help the animal.

"Maisie." The hardness in her tone caused her friend to whirl around. "I'll finish that bread. You go tell Leonard to keep that dog alive as long as he can. You tell him that if he comes by in two hours, I'll have something for her, and half of one of my fried chickens for your dinner." She wanted to go herself, but knew that Papa would punish her if he found out she'd been to the barns, and with all the hands out there—DeVille's included—she didn't want to risk it today.

Eyes wide, Maisie was already wiping her hands down on her apron. "What are you thinkin' now, Ella?"

"That it'd be a real shame to let that sweet animal die because of some fools who can't have fun without hurting another creature." Was she speaking about the Miller Ranch hands, or her own stepsisters? Ella wasn't sure anymore, honestly. But she was already pulling out bandages from the cabinet in the corner, and trying to figure out what she could make to keep the pup's strength up. Maybe an extra chicken? Lord knew that her fried chicken was tasty enough to heal a grown man… maybe it'd work on dogs too? "I know Leonard can't work miracles, but you tell him that if there's any way that he can stay around the barn today instead of going out on the range, I sure would appreciate it if he did everything he could to keep that dog alive."

Smiling sadly, Maisie took the bundle from Ella. "You know he thinks the world of you, and so do I, girl. You finish up the biscuits for those fools' dinner, and me an' my man will make sure that dog's still alive when you come by with the food." But then her expression turned serious. "But no doctor is gunna fix up an animal, and you ain't a healer. Best we can do is keep her comfortable 'til she passes. *You* can't fix her."

"No." Ella felt her shoulders straighten in determination. She thought about Ian, with his haunted eyes and his gentleness with his dogs. She thought about Papa's ultimatum and her stepsisters' cruelty. She thought about that poor animal, dying alone out behind the barn while Ella's "guards" were drinking themselves stupid. And she decided that nothing her stepfather could do to her would be worse than what she'd do to herself, if she let the pup die without trying to help her. "No, but I know someone who can."

July third was hard, as always. In the past, it'd been the day that Ian retreated to his apartment with a full bottle of whiskey, and tried not to remember. Twelve years ago today had been the day that his world changed forever. He remembered lying there among the boulders, staring up at the Pennsylvania sky — clear and open and blue — feeling his life soak into the pebbly dirt under him. He remembered hands, clutching and pulling him towards safety, but that they didn't matter, as long as that sky was above him. He remembered the stretcher, and knowing that he was dying, and saying goodbye to his parents, and praying. He remembered the doctor bending over him with the saw, and then he didn't remember anything else.

He'd woken up with one less leg, weak as a baby, and angry at not being allowed to die. Angry at being forced to relearn how to walk, how to live. Angry at the war, at the world. And then to get the letter from Mother, explaining that Uncle Albert had been killed at Vicksburg on July third, and that Father's heart had given out when he'd gotten word about his brother's death and son's maiming on the same day... Ian's anger had warred with his despair, and then both gave way to determination.

Sitting in his armchair, listening to the rain beating against the window, Ian just stared at the amber liquid in the glass clutched in his hand. He hadn't taken a single drink, but he was already maudlin. But yet, this year didn't seem as bad as last year, or the year before. Maybe the old saying was true; maybe Time *did* heal all wounds.

Or *maybe* he should just man up and admit the truth to himself; he was a different person than he was last year. Than last month, even. He had... friends now. He had a place in a community that he hadn't even dreamed of, last July third. Last year, last month, he'd just been surviving, living week-to-week and trying to keep his parents' dream of owning a mercantile alive. The dogs who were currently stretched around the room in various states of repose had been his only reason for living. He hadn't been thinking of the future, then.

Now, though… now he felt like he actually *belonged* someplace. Like he had people who might notice if he wasn't at church, or didn't join the now-weekly poker game at the Gingerbread House. All it had taken was a few nights of *not* going back to the shop after dinner at Spratt's, of going outside of his… his comfort zone. But his "zone" had now expanded, and included Everland and Everland's people. He hadn't realized just how secluded he was, until he wasn't.

Over the last weeks, Max had introduced him to most of the townspeople, and they'd introduced him to everyone else. He'd known many of them by sight, watching them pass by his shop, but now he knew them by name, and knew their laughter and stories and homes. It hadn't hurt that he'd had the support of Max DeVille, probably the most popular man in town.

Ian had even accepted a few invitations to dinner, and had been surprised how much he'd enjoyed himself. It wasn't until after that he'd realized every single invitation had come from a family with an eligible daughter, who'd done her best to entice him with baked goods and witty conversation. Maybe now that he was a member of the community, these young ladies were seeing him with new eyes, like Max had said. Looking at the whole him, rather than just his missing leg?

But no matter how tasty the meals, or how pretty the ladies, none of them could compare to Ella. None of the dinners matched a simple shared picnic of fried chicken, none of the ladies had the same strength and compassion that he'd seen in her, and none of them had seen him as Ella had seen him, that very first time.

Sighing, Ian finally took a drink of the whiskey, and winced as it burned the back of his throat and stomach. Maybe he should've eaten dinner tonight, after all. But he'd lingered in the store, reluctant to face anyone else today, and then the thunder had started, and he'd just called in the dogs and retired upstairs to get ready for bed. It was late enough now that it'd be full dark outside even without the storm that had apparently decided to hover directly over this corner of the Wyoming Territory.

The lightening had moved off, at least, but the occasional burst of thunder still startled Vick enough to lift her heard and *wuff*. Manny was actually curled up on Ian's lap, her shaking subsided now that his hand rested heavily on the little dog's back. Shiloh always slept through storms, as if knowing he had nothing to fear, and judging from the canine snoring coming from the pile of blankets in the corner, tonight was no different.

But tonight was different for *Ian*. Tonight was the first July third in twelve years that he didn't want to get drunk to forget. Instead, he found himself staring at the little amber trails down the inside of his glass, and *remembering* her. He didn't want to forget her.

He'd taken old Mrs. Zapato's advice, and made himself part of the community. He'd made friends, and had been accepted, and even courted. But the whole time he'd been looking for a pair of turquoise eyes and coal-black hair. And he hadn't found her.

Weeks of dreaming about her — her touch, her smile, her kiss — meant that he wasn't likely to forget what she looked like. But he'd looked at every young woman in town — even the harlots who hung around the Gingerbread House's main room, and had asked Max and Ox for their help, and… nothing. No one knew of a young woman who sewed and cooked and cleaned for her sisters, and he was beginning to wonder if he'd dreamed her entirely.

But he couldn't have dreamed the perfection of her smile, or the shock that had gone through his entire body when they'd touched. He couldn't have dreamed her compassion towards his crippled dog, or the way that she was impressed by the way he'd arranged his store to accommodate his own disability. He couldn't have dreamed someone as perfect and gentle and *strong* as Ella.

Ella, whoever she was.

Ian scowled and took another drink, scratching Manny's ears when the dog shifted slightly. Maybe he *had* imagined her. She hadn't been back in weeks, and Ian hadn't been able to find her. Tomorrow was the big Independence Day celebration—he'd donated a big barrel of pickles for the picnic—and maybe it was time to smile back at some of those young ladies. He'd told Max that he didn't intend to bid on any of the baskets, and he sure couldn't join in any of the dancing, but that didn't mean that he couldn't laugh and joke and try his damnedest to impress a pretty lady.

When was the last time he'd done that? Back before the war, probably, when he'd been young and full of hope for the future. Maybe it was time, again.

At first, he thought that the rain had just picked up, rattling against his window. But then Shiloh lifted his head and growled, and Ian realized that Vick was staring at the door and Manny was staring at the window. Then the rattling against the panes came again, and Ian realized it wasn't rain; it was something harder. Putting the whiskey on the small table beside the chair, he lifted Manny to the floor, and using the back of the chair and the wall, heaved himself over to the window. It was dark enough that he wondered what exactly he was hoping to see… and then a flash of distant lightening lit up a figure standing in the alley behind his store.

He only saw it for a moment, but that was all he'd needed. A rain-drenched woman in a dress, holding a bundle, pale face staring up at him, an oilcloth covering her hair and shoulders. She was lifting another handful of the pebbles from the alley to hurl at his window, when he waved to let her know he saw her.

She'd come back to him.

Without bothering to pull on a shirt—not even sure that he believed she was real—Ian threw himself towards the rail that lined the living room. He'd left his crutch downstairs, knowing that he could get around fine in his own house, and even now he didn't regret it. Shifting himself into the stairway, he gripped both railings, picked up his foot, and swung himself down the stairs at a record rate. At the bottom, rather than turning left to go through the store room and into the shop, he turned towards the alley door, the one that he'd locked tonight, like every night.

Taking a deep breath, Ian laid a hand on the latch. This was it. Either he opened the door and she was there, or she wasn't, and then he went back upstairs and checked the amount of whiskey he'd drunk. He opened the door.

She was real.

Ella was standing on the small stoop behind his shop, the oilcloth around her shoulders, and covered in mud to her knees. Her eyes were puffy, like she'd been crying, and the bundle she was clutching to her chest was dirty and bloody. She looked like a woman in desperate need of a prince, and Ian's chest expanded as he took a deep breath.

She was real, she was here, and he was ready to do absolutely anything he could to help her.

CHAPTER EIGHT

He wasn't wearing a shirt. *He wasn't wearing a shirt.* Vaguely, Ella was aware of the rain pelting her shoulders and scalp, and the heavy breathing of the pup in her arms, and the distant sound of thunder... but all she could focus on was the expanse of skin in front of her. Goodness, his chest just stretched on and on, didn't it? Unconsciously, she licked her lips, her eyes following the curve of his shoulders down his thick arms, wondering why she felt so light-headed.

Oh yes, *breathe.*

She sucked in a deep breath, and tried not to cough when the much-needed air hit her lungs. Dragging her attention back to his face, she saw his smile. He wasn't smiling at her like he was laughing at her inattention; rather, that he was just happy to see her. His chest may have stolen her breath, but his smile stopped her heart. Seeing him, his pale eyes lit with pleasure just because *she* was there... well, it was enough to make any girl weak-kneed.

No wonder she'd fallen in love with him; he was the first man who'd ever looked at her like that.

There was no way of knowing how long they stood there, staring at one another. Eventually a particularly loud crack of thunder caused the dog in her arms to jump and let out a pitiful whine—whether from fear or pain, Ella wasn't sure. Ian's eyes dropped to the bundle she was holding, and she saw his rust-colored brows draw in over his glasses. Bracing himself on the door handle and the wall, he swung himself back out of the doorway.

"You'd better come in, Ella."

Her name on his lips was beautiful, enticing. As she stepped into his domain, she thought that she might follow that voice anywhere.

But soon she was dripping in the back foyer of his shop, shivering despite the heat, clutching the pup against her. She could see the entrance to the storage room through the door, and the stairs that presumably led up to the apartment he'd mentioned. His hip was braced against the wall by the stairs, and his arms were crossed in front of that magnificent chest.

"I'm not going to say I'm not thrilled to see you, Ella, but you picked an odd time to come visiting."

There was no censure in his voice—only laughter—but she was quick to blurt, "I need you."

Was it her imagination, or did his expression soften? "Anything you need." It wasn't an offer; it was a promise.

Oh good Heavens, there went her knees again. Ella had to swallow, and look down at the pup she carried, before she could still her treacherous heart and remember why she was here. "I found her. Well, I didn't find her, I knew where she was, but she was hiding. She needs your help. She needs someone's help, and I can't help her, and I didn't know who else could, and then I remembered Manny, and I thought..."

Ella stopped herself, and took a deep breath, knowing that she was completely mangling the explanation, but unable to help it. She slowly peeled back the now-soaked towel she'd hoped would protect the pup, and the animal let out a faint whine when the light from the lamp hit its face. She risked a glance up at Ian, wondering what he thought of her boldness.

He was frowning down at the dog. Slowly, gently, he reached out a hand to stroke the pup's head, and his frown deepened when she whined again. Ella could tell that he was being careful not to startle her or frighten her any more than she already was. The animal's breathing quickened, but she made no move to squirm away; Ella hoped it was because she trusted Ian, rather than because she was too weak to move.

"I think," Ian met her eyes, "that you'd better tell me everything." She let her relief show in her face, and knew that he'd seen it when his frown faded. "Let's get her upstairs—you'll have to carry her." Of course. He needed both of his hands free to navigate the stairs. "But first, I think that you'd better get out of those wet clothes."

…What? He wanted her to … to what? To take her clothes off? Here? In his shop?

Maybe her horror showed, because his lips quirked upwards. "I meant, take off your boots and stockings down here." He pulled the oilcloth from her shoulders, and hung it on a peg by the door, where it dripped onto a small rug. Then, before her heartbeat had even returned to normal, he was holding out his arms towards the pup. "You'd better give her to me."

The idea of removing *any* article of clothing in his presence was horrifying and thrilling all at once. But she couldn't very well stomp through his apartment in ruined boots, not after the kindness he'd showed her already. So, with a sigh that acknowledged the inevitability of revealing her imperfect skin to this perfect prince, she handed him the dog, and bent over.

Luckily, he kept up a murmured litany of comfort to the animal, as he peeled back the towel to look at her injuries, and Ella was almost able to pretend that he was ignoring the way her ankles, and then her knees, were exposed to the gas light.

When she stood barefoot and self-conscious before him, he just smiled slightly, and had her leave her stockings draped over the railing to dry. Then he handed the dog back to her and turned to lift himself up the stairs. She noticed the way his eyes lingered on her worn—now-muddy—work boots, and tried to tamp down the burn of shame that made her toes curls under her damp, frayed skirt.

He led the way to his apartment, and Ella had to swallow down the fierce thrill of longing that swept through her when she saw his cozy home. Despite the fact that it should've been hot and muggy in the July storm, the little space felt welcoming. He had a large armchair beside one of the windows, and a small table stood next to it with a half-full bottle of whiskey. A kitchen table was pushed up against one wall, with a single chair under it, and the kitchen was small and serviceable and utterly wonderful. A door on the other side of the large black stove — obviously the source of heat in winter — led to what must be his bedroom. Everything was strategically placed so that he could support himself using only his arms, and railings lined most of the walls. There were frames on a few shelves, a large braided rug on the floor, cheerful curtains around the windows, and all-in-all, it looked like the sort of home Ella had always dreamed of having.

It wasn't until he cleared his throat that she realized she was standing in his front door, staring. Blushing, she stepped into his apartment, making sure that the muddy hem of her skirt didn't make too much of a mess. He gestured towards the kitchen table as he moved towards the bedroom. "Why don't you sit down, and put her on the table? Try to clean off as much of the mud as possible, and you hold her while I look her over."

Pleased to have some direction, Ella hurried to the table. The towel hadn't kept the pup dry, but at least it had kept off the worst of the mud. She whispered soothingly as she cleaned the dried blood from the animal's coat as well as she could, and it seemed to help. She was so intent on keeping the animal calm that Ian's sudden presence beside her — he put down the small box of supplies by her elbow and pulled up a tall stool from the kitchen — made her jump. He was wearing a shirt, now, but it wasn't tucked in or buttoned all the way up, and he was rolling the sleeves up to reveal those magnificent forearms when she finally gathered the courage to look up at him.

He just nodded down at her and settled himself on the stool. It looked like he was used to dragging the stool around the house, and she supposed that he must have difficulty standing for too long. Tugging on the towel, he pulled the dog towards him, and Ella shifted so that she could keep stroking the animal's head. "Why don't you tell me what happened?"

As he carefully examined the dog's wounds — which still made Ella cringe when she saw them — she told him the story of the dog-fight and how she'd bribed Leonard to hide the pup, and keep her safe. She told how, after dinner, she cleaned up and told her family that she was retiring early, but really snuck out to the barns and past her stepfather's sleeping men, and finally found the poor creature, torn-up and in desperate pain. She told how she didn't know how to save her, but how she'd hoped Ian would, and how she was halfway back to the house with the dog wrapped in the towel when the storm started. Even that hadn't been enough to deter her; not when she was determined to save the animal.

"Hmmmm," Ian agreed, bent over the pup's side with a cloth and some kind of liquid that made her whine when he dabbed it on her wound. "You could've been struck by lightning. And you probably ruined your boots."

"Honestly, I was more worried about the dog. I've visited her since she was born, and loved watching her play. I was just so *furious* when I'd heard what they'd done!"

"Dog fighting is a cruel sport." She heard his anger in the tightness of his reply.

"It's not the first time the DeVille hands have come over to make trouble with my stepfather's men."

The moment the words left her mouth, Ella bit her tongue. *Oh, shoot!* Had she given away too much? Did he know who her stepfather was? Judging from the way his hands stilled momentarily, and the muscles in his forearm tightened, he'd noticed her blunder, and was trying to place the clue she'd just accidentally revealed.

But all he said was, "I recently met Max DeVille," in a neutral tone.

Oh dear. How to respond? She stared down at the pup's head, and continued to stroke her ears. "I've never met the family." She wasn't allowed to.

"Hmmmm." Was all he said to that, and Ella hoped that meant that he was too intent on the dog's injuries to follow through on the questioning. When he threaded a needle and began to stitch the animal's wounds together, Ella breathed a little sigh of relief. He'd asked about her family last time too, and she'd refrained from telling him because she was ashamed. But now, with Papa's threat hanging over her, she couldn't tell him for his own good.

Ian had worked so hard to make Crowne's Mercantile a successful business, and he didn't have the same standing in the community that Papa did. Edmund Miller was a wealthy man, and if he and Roy DeVille agreed on something, they could work together to bring Ian down. She wasn't about to allow that to happen, not if she had any say over the matter. And the only thing that she could do was make sure that Papa didn't have a reason to work against Ian. He could never know that she'd snuck past the men he'd set to guard her tonight to see Ian; could never hear their names linked.

She cared about Ian too much to ever let that happen.

By the time that he was finished stitching the dog up, Ella was breathing normally again, confident in her decision. Ian was washing the dog's fur out when he spoke again. "What's her name?"

"I don't think she has one."

He glanced at her, a flash of green behind the glass. "She's not your dog?" The surprise in his voice made her cautious when she answered.

She couldn't drop any more hints, or let him know that she lived on a prosperous cattle ranch.

"No. I've just been visiting her from time to time."

"Well, I can wrap her up well enough for you to take her home, since the storm's stopped." Sure enough, Ella realized that she hadn't heard any rain against the windows. At least tomorrow's celebration wouldn't be ruined. Not that it mattered, since she couldn't go.

"Actually, I was hoping that I could leave her here, with you. If you don't mind. You'd get to name her."

Ian patted the dog softly, and sat back on his stool, eying her seriously. She wasn't sure why this pup mattered so much to her; all she knew was that if she returned the animal to the Miller Ranch, she was unlikely to survive, and Ella might have to explain who stitched her up.

But the longer than Ian stared at her, the deeper she felt him in her own soul, and the more she understood that this wasn't about the dog. This was about her. About him. About *them*.

"On one condition."

Ian watched her swallow, the lamplight playing across the pale skin of her neck as her muscles contracted. He could tell that he'd made her nervous, and knew that she was thinking of the slip-up she'd made a while ago. So focused on the poor dog's injuries, he hadn't been able to devote much of his mind to the riddle she'd posed, but he fully intended to.

To his surprise, though, she accepted his challenge. "What's your condition?"

He smiled slowly. "That you come back and visit her." Visit the dog, not him. See? Everything is perfectly reasonable here.

But when her face fell, his stomach dropped too. He hadn't realized how strongly he'd been hoping she'd say yes, but it was obvious that she was going to say no. Rather than letting her see his disappointment, Ian shifted forward off the stool, picked it up, and used it to hobble towards the kitchen counter. With his back to her, he washed his hands in the basin, and tried not to swallow down the hurt her denial had caused.

"I'm sorry, Ian." Her voice was small, weak. Nothing like her. "I… I can't."

"You can't, or you won't?" His hands, resting on either side of the basin, fisted, and he stared at the wall in front of him.

"I can't." God, he hated how pitiful she sounded. He would do anything to take her fear away.

Ian let his head drop, felt the pull along his neck and down his spine, and exhaled slowly. She was *here*. She was in his home, talking to him, and she was *real*. He wasn't going to let her go without a fight, this time.

"I dreamed about you, you know." He hadn't intended to admit that. Why had the confession slipped out?

He held his breath until he heard her quiet response. "Me too."

Feeling like the world was somehow balancing out again, but not exactly sure how, Ian turned to face her, propping his hip against the counter. He folded his arms across his chest, and felt a thrill when her eyes followed the movement and lingered on his forearms. "You dream about me?"

She was still staring at his arms, and Ian resisted the urged to flex his muscles. "Yes." She swallowed and lifted those gorgeous clear eyes to his. "Every night."

Every night. The same as him. What were the odds? "In your dreams, what are we doing?"

Was it his imagination, or did she pale even further? "We're talking."

"Just talking?"

He could tell that she was uncomfortable with the topic, from the jerky movements she made as she stroked the young dog's head, but he wouldn't let her look away. He held her gaze, willing her to answer him, to stay with him. Always.

"Sometimes…" She swallowed again, and her voice dropped to a whisper. "Sometimes we're kissing."

Well now… Ian raised one of his brows, as if he didn't believe her. "Kissing, eh?" In his dreams, they were doing a heck of a lot more than kissing, but he'd take her admission for what it was worth. "Just kissing?"

Had he thought that she was pale? Suddenly color bloomed in her cheeks, bright enough to rival her lips. "Just kissing." And he knew that she was lying.

"In these dreams of yours, when we're kissing…" Was it his imagination, or was she leaning forward slightly in her chair? Her lips were parted, her turquoise-blue eyes were wide, and in that moment, he loved everything about her. "What were we wearing?"

He had to press his lips together to keep the laughter from escaping at her reaction. She sat up quickly, and must've dug her fingers into the dog's fur or something, because it gave a strangled yelp she didn't even seem to notice. Her cheeks pinked even more, and she looked ready to bolt. Ian took pity on her. "Because in *my* dreams, we're not wearing much of anything at all."

She bolted. With a strangled noise, Ella launched herself out of the chair, and took a few jerky steps towards the window, as if not sure why she was headed there, but needing to move. He felt safe letting a few satisfied chuckles escape. He'd rattled her, all right, but it'd been the truth. Even now, he had to shift his hips slightly to get comfortable in his own trousers. Even the memory of those dreams were potent.

He watched her shoulders expand slightly with each breath, the thin material of her worn shirt still slightly damp. Everything she was wearing was slightly damp, in fact. The oilcloth that she'd thrown over herself and the dog hadn't done a perfect job, but at least she wasn't soaked. His gaze traveled down her frame, his experienced shopkeeper's eye taking in the out-of-date cut of the blouse she wore, the ragged hem of her skirt, and her bare feet under it. Her boots — the same pair that she'd worn the last times she'd visited — had been old to begin with, and being soaked through and slogged through mud probably wasn't going to help them. He thought of them, sitting beside the back door to his shop, and thought of her trying to put them back on to walk out of his life again.

He wasn't going to let her do that. This time, when she walked out on him, she'd be obligated enough to come back. Ian was willing to do anything to keep her in his life.

But for now, he made small talk as they cleaned up together, making her laugh with stories of other dogs he'd fixed up. They discussed the pup's prognosis, and she seemed relieved that it would not just live, but live well. He called Shiloh and Manny and Vick over to meet the new pup, and he and Ella fussed over the animals for sitting so quietly and patiently during the operation. Ian boiled water for some tea, and shared it with her at the kitchen table.

Being here, with her and the dogs, felt *right.* Seeing her smiling and laughing with him, scratching Vick behind the ears while she sipped her tea, felt *right*. Making the pup a new bed to keep her safe and secure, and watching Ella fuss over her while they worked together… it all felt *right*.

And Ian knew: This is what he wanted. Forever. He wanted her here with him, seeing him for who he really was. He wanted her compassion, her industry, her loyalty, in his life. He wanted to protect her, to provide for her, to come home every evening to her and the dogs and maybe, someday, a child, a full home that she would help him build. He wanted *her*.

He was going to marry her, and keep her forever. And he knew how to do it.

When, at almost midnight, Ella finally said that she had to go, Ian didn't fight her. He just gestured for her to follow him, and he swung down the stairs to the back foyer. Rather than letting her out the door, though, he turned to the store room, and she picked up the lamp and followed.

He knew exactly what he was looking for; it had come in last week's delivery. Sure enough, in the ladies' ready-wear section, he pulled them out. Holding onto the shelves with one hand, he turned to Ella.

She stared down at the shoes in his hand. They were black, and unadorned, and not at all the kind of thing that a suitor should give the woman he was rapidly realizing he loved. But when she turned breathless, bright eyes up to him, he knew that he'd made the right choice.

"For me?"

"Your boots are ruined. Leave them here, and I'll do what I can to fix them up for you." Dry them, scrape them, reshape them — if possible — and oil them. Maybe he could take them to Micah Zapato, who'd taken over his grandfather's cobbling business. "This way you don't have to walk home in wet boots."

Hesitantly, she reached out and touched one of the shoes, running her finger down the smooth dark leather. They were serviceable, with a simple sort of beauty. But her beauty — when she smiled up at him — was anything but simple.

"You're giving me shoes?"

Ian was hit with a wave of self-doubt. What if this wasn't what she needed? What she wanted? He hadn't courted a woman before; what if *shoes* were a terrible choice of gifts? "I… Do you want them? You don't have to take them."

Her fingers stroked along the insole, and Ian shuddered, remember those fingers doing the same to his skin in his dreams. "I think…" She inhaled slowly. "I love them. No one…" She looked up, and met his eyes, and he was done. "No one has *ever* given me such a wonderful gift."

If she let him, he'd give her gifts — even more wonderful than this — for the rest of her life. He felt like his heart was in his throat when he asked, "You'll take them?"

Their fingers brushed when she wrapped her hands around the shoes, and the thrill shot up his arm, as always. What was it about this woman's touch that could affect him so? Ian didn't care; as long as he had plenty of more chances to touch her.

"Thank you, Ian."

Anything for you. He couldn't make his throat work.

"I can't pay you for them, but I will return them as soon as possible."

"No!" He managed to choke it out. "No," he repeated, softer. "They're a gift. But..." He wrapped his free hand around hers, which was still holding the shoes. "But I need to see you again. Please." She looked away, and he felt his stomach clench. "Please tell me your family name. Tell me where I can find you."

He didn't care that he was pleading. He didn't care that it made him sound weak, desperate; when it came to her, he *was* desperate. He didn't care about anything, as long as he had a way to find her again. He hoped that the shoes would provide that opportunity.

But as she pulled her hands from his, he was afraid that he'd lost her yet again. "I can't, Ian." She clutched the shoes to her chest. "For your sake, I can't tell you my name."

She'd mentioned her stepfather earlier; was he the one who had this mysterious hold over her? Was he the one who was preventing her from even sharing her name, preventing them from working towards a future? It was her voice—sad and defeated—that told him she wanted to confess, but couldn't. Ian wanted to fix it, to make it better, but he warned himself to take it slowly.

So he touched her; he couldn't stop himself. He stroked one finger down her smooth cheek, and imagined what it would feel like to cup that cheek, to pull her closer to him. To kiss her. He watched her close her eyes on her shudder, and knew that she was as affected by their connection as he was.

"I won't push you, Ella. But promise that you'll come back to me."

"I… I can't." He barely heard her whisper. "I shouldn't have even come here tonight, but I had to see…"

"Promise me. If you don't, if I don't know that I'll see you again soon, I'll go crazy. I'll follow you tonight, I swear I will."

She glanced up at him then, probably to see if he was teasing her, and he caught and held her turquoise gaze. He kept his expression neutral, and nodded. "Just imagine me stumping after you, in the mud. My crutch will probably get stuck and I'll fall."

Was that a hint of a smile there, on her lips? Her eyes were carefully serious when she finally said, "I would hate to be the cause of that." And there wasn't an ounce of pity in her gaze. She accepted him as he was.

He nodded solemnly again. "I wouldn't have a leg to stand on."

That did it. She burst into laughter, and *God* was she beautiful, all lit up like that. Ian vowed then and there to make her laugh as much as possible. Ella deserved to have laughter and fun and beauty and ease.

She was still chuckling when she touched his arm. "I'll come back."

"Promise?"

"I shouldn't, but yes. I can't imagine not seeing you again."

He shuddered theatrically. "Thank God."

"I wouldn't want you to feel obligated to come after me."

"Come tomorrow." He wasn't sure where the demand came from, why he made it. "Come to the picnic tomorrow. I can't promise to dance with you," he hadn't danced in twelve years, "but I want to see you. To put you on my arm and parade you in front of Everland and show them how beautiful you are."

It was the wrong thing to say. Her gaze shuttered again, and she drew away — physically and emotionally. He *watched* the joy drain out of her eyes, and wondered at the sorrow that replaced it. He hated feeling so helpless to help her. "I'm sorry. I shouldn't have…"

"Thank you very much for the shoes, Ian." She sat down on the bottom step and made quick work of pulling on her stockings and the simple black shoes. "They fit perfectly."

Of course they did. That was his job; knowing what goods each person needed. For instance, he knew that she needed healing, peace, and laughter. And right now, he couldn't give her any of that.

Then she was standing at his door, a good ten feet from him, her hand on the jamb. "Thank you for taking care of the pup."

He didn't want her to leave on a sour note. "You sure you won't help me name her?"

She shook her head, sadly. "No. That's for you to do. But…" She opened the door, and backed towards it. "Promise me something."

"Anything."

"Don't name her after a battle, Ian. That's your past." And then she was gone.

Ian stood in his store room for a while, thinking about what she'd said. For twelve years, he'd been caught up in the memories of that one day. His life had changed forever on July third, and he'd hadn't let it change again. He'd named his dogs—his closest companions—for those battles, to remind himself of what he'd lost, and what he was.

But this July third, things were different. The town of Everland had accepted him. He had a place to belong, and he had a mysterious woman to devote himself to. He had hope for the future; a future that didn't care how many legs he had.

And suddenly, he knew what he was going to name the tiny black pup sleeping upstairs on his kitchen table.

On the way home, Ella took off the shoes and the stockings. They were beautiful, and far too precious to her to get covered in mud. Perhaps, tomorrow or the next day or next week, her stepsisters would notice them and hound her until she had to make up a lie about them, but for now, they were the most valuable thing she owned. She clutched them to her chest as she walked out of the town, not caring if that meant that her hem dragged in the mud instead.

He'd given her shoes. No one had ever given her something like that before. He'd seen something that she'd needed, and freely gifted it. No wonder she loved him.

If only there was some way that she could show him. If only there was some way for them to be together. That pretty yellow dress she'd been making would've been perfect for tomorrow's parade and picnic. She could've held her head high as she walked into town behind her sisters. She could've felt comfortable smiling and laughing and sharing with Ian.

But she wasn't going. Could never go. Her stepsisters and stepfather had made it perfectly clear that she was never, *ever* to go into town, or see Ian again.

Ella stopped still in the road, a half-hour from the Miller Ranch. Papa had forbidden her to go into town, or to see Ian, but she had. She'd defied him, for the sake of the pup. For her own sake. She'd *needed* to see Ian, and that need had been greater than her fear of Papa. And hadn't she just tonight, there in his store room, promised that she'd see him again? Promised that she'd find a way to come back?

She loved Ian more than she feared Papa. And Ian wanted to see her tomorrow at the picnic. It wouldn't be easy; she'd have to come in her drab blue work dress, and she'd have to walk the whole way, and she'd have to find a way to sneak past her family and Papa's guards... but maybe.

Just maybe.

Remembering the way Sibyl used to wish on stars, and how she'd force Ella to go along with her and wish — or pretend to wish — as well, she took a deep breath. Throwing her head back, staring up at the huge Wyoming sky, Ella inhaled deeply.

The storm had passed and the clouds had cleared. *There!* There was the brightest star, sparkling down like it was made just for her. She resisted the urge to close her eyes, and instead focused on that one star as hard as she could.

And she wished.

Please. Oh please. I want to go to the picnic tomorrow. I want to be with him. Forever.

CHAPTER NINE

Wishing on stars was stupid. It meant that she thought that they were magic, but magic wasn't real. And it definitely didn't work. As Ella stood on the front porch of Papa's grand ranch house, watching him drive his fancy buggy into town, her stepsisters laughing and preening, and in the back of her mind, Ella knew that magic wasn't real.

The morning had been worse than she'd thought; Mabel was up early, demanding that Ella starch the latest lace addition to her dress, and then Eunice insisted on having her second-best stockings darned, so that she could wear those instead of the white ones. Ella managed to do both, in between frying the chicken and pulling the oatmeal cookies out of the oven, and then it was time to start on her sisters' hair. Luckily, Maisie was an excellent hair-dresser, and the Miller daughters might not have liked associating with her, but they loved her designs.

So it wasn't even noon yet, and Ella was drained. She'd gotten home well after midnight, and then been woken before dawn to start on breakfast and the food for the picnic baskets. Her shoulders and legs ached, and her heart ached too.

She missed him. She'd seen Ian only last night, but already missed him, and mourned the lost opportunity of spending the day with him. Now that her family had left, though, she was planning on crawling back onto her pallet and sleeping for a few more hours. It was the only way to forget about last night's stupidity.

Wishing on a star? Honestly, where had that ever gotten her?

But despite her intentions, she was still standing there on the porch, watching her family disappear over the same ridge where she and her mother had stood all those years ago, looking down on their new house. She was still standing there when their cloud of dust dissipated, and she was still standing there when a new cloud of dust appeared.

Ella had just decided that the newcomer was probably a group of cowboys from DeVille's place, come to see Papa's hands — despite almost everyone being in town for the picnic — when the shape resolved itself into a stagecoach. And not just any stagecoach; it was a gaily-painted one, streamers hanging off the top and colorful swirls covering the sides. It was the oddest-looking vehicle that Ella had ever seen, and it was heading for the house, rather than the barns.

When the coach pulled to a stop right in front of her, Ella decided that the driver was even odder-looking that her conveyance. The woman was young and beautiful, with bright red hair pulled back under a purple headscarf. She wore the reform bloomers that had gone out of style a few decades before, tucked into gleaming black boots, and she was draped in golden jewelry — necklaces, bracelets and even the multiple tiny rings adoring her ears all clanged merrily as she set the brake and climbed down from her perch.

Ella realized that she was watching with her mouth agape, and quickly tried to remember her manners. It wasn't easy. When the tired-looking horse on the left turned its head to give her an entirely too-knowing look, Ella shook her head and hurried down the steps. The woman had opened the coach's doors, and was pulling out a large white box.

To Ella's surprise, the strange-looking woman—up close, Ella could see that she had genuinely *purple* eyes—handed her the flat box. "A delivery, my dear." She had a strange accent, musical and mysterious.

Accepting the lighter-than-it-looked box, Ella tried not to let her confusion show. They'd never—as far as she knew—had a box delivered directly to the ranch. Anything that her sisters had ordered had been delivered to Everland, and then one of the hands brought it back here. A direct delivery, and from such an odd delivery person, was new.

The label—printed in a lovely flowing script—indicated that the package was for "E. Miller." It looked like one of the boxes that the fancy dressmakers back east shipped their gowns in; apparently Eunice had ordered something that Ella hadn't known about.

"What's your name, dear?"

"Ella."

"Well, Ella, I'd say that your new dress has arrived. Let's see how it looks!"

Flustered at the woman's directness, and not wanting to be rude, Ella shook her head and took a step back, still holding the box. "No, I'm sorry. You see, my sister's name is Eunice. This is for her, I'm sure."

"Nonsense!" To Ella's horror, the woman took a step towards her and lifted the top of the box to reveal the thin paper. "This is for E. Miller, and you're an E. Miller, aren't you?" *Am I?* "So this is for you." The woman's reasoning wasn't sound; Ella had never really been a Miller, since her mother married Papa after—

And then she wasn't thinking at all, because the woman had pulled out the most beautiful turquoise gown, trimmed in the same black velvet ribbon that Ella had admired so deeply at Crowne's Mercantile all those weeks ago. As the woman lifted the dress by its shoulders, Ella felt the box slip from her numb fingers. The gown was an elegant cut, simple in its design, and made to accentuate the wearer's curves. Ella's palms itched to run down the bodice, to check the layers of the bustle, to caress the velvet trimmings. If she'd ever been allowed to design a dress, from scratch, for herself, she wouldn't have had the audacity to design something this wonderfully perfect.

It wasn't until she heard the woman's chuckle that she realized she'd stopped breathing. Taking in a frantic gulp of air, she met the strange woman's eyes. Her expression softened. "Trust me, my dear. This dress is for you."

This dress is for you, sweetheart. It was something she remembered Mama saying to her for her sixth birthday, and then once again after they'd moved here to Wyoming. And since then, no one else had said it. She'd made do with hand-me-downs and scraps, and no one had ever given her anything.

Until last night. Until Ian gave her those lovely new shoes.

Ian. He'd be at the picnic today. The picnic that she'd longed to go to. The picnic that she'd asked the wishing star to be able to attend.

Maybe the wishing star sent her a chance, after all? Her family was gone, and here was a dress, and if she asked politely, maybe the woman might even give her a ride back into town. Riding with her would make it much easier to sneak away from any unlucky cowboys who'd been left on the ranch to guard her.

Taking a deep breath, Ella straightened her shoulders. "Are you going back to Everland, ma'am?" When the red-headed woman smiled and nodded, Ella plucked up her courage. "Would you consider taking me with you?"

"Of course! I'll take a moment to feed and water my horses, if you don't mind the delay?"

Gratefully, Ella smiled. "That is perfect, actually. I'll be back soon." She didn't quite snatch the dress from the woman's hands, but it was close. Still, the stranger was smiling when Ella darted up the stairs and into the house.

In the kitchen, Ella quickly stripped out of her worn work dress and pulled on the new turquoise gown. It fit like a glove, like it had been made for her. Even the yellow dress, which had been the first thing that Ella had made for herself in a long while, hadn't fit this well. This gown had been made by a master, and Ella had the very brazen desire to preen in front of the mirror upstairs. There was no time, though.

And no time for elaborate hairstyles — Maisie was already back at her house with Leonard, no doubt preparing to go into town too. So Ella just pulled the pins out of the sedate bun she normally wore, and reveled in the feel of her curls — still slightly damp from last night's adventure — cascading down her back. For the finishing touch, she pulled on the shoes that Ian had given her.

They went perfectly with her new gown. She felt like a princess, on her way to see her prince.

Not knowing what the day would bring, Ella hurried to pack a little bundle of oatmeal cookies. She'd been planning on having them with her lunch, as a special treat, but she'd better bring them with her in case she didn't get to eat. And maybe the mysterious woman would like some in appreciation for the ride?

Ella hurried out the door, feeling like a different woman. And judging from the way the stranger smiled, she looked like one, too. The woman didn't say anything when she held the coach door open for Ella to climb in, but did accept a cookie with a kind nod. Then the door was shut and the horses were *cluck*ed into motion, and Ella was being carried off to the picnic in an actual *stagecoach*. She felt like a princess with some sort of secret godmother!

When they reached the outskirts of Everland, the reality of what Ella was doing suddenly sunk in, and she considered begging the woman to stop and let her out. Then she thought of Ian's expression last night, when he'd practically begged her to see him again, and thought of the way his touch made her feel and the way he'd held her in her dreams last night. And knew that she could do this. She had to do this.

There was no one on the streets, but the woman directed her horses down the main street and to the large fair grounds west of the town.

Apparently they'd missed the Independence Day parade, but the picnic was in full swing. As they grew closer, Ella could smell the roasting pig, and hear the band and the calls of the townspeople. Mr. Smith, the Mayor, was standing on a small bandstand, calling to a crowd about something-or-other, and children were darting this way and that throughout the clumps of people. Dogs were barking, men were shouting, women were laughing, and Ella craned her neck, looking for a rust-colored head amid the crush.

He'd be here. She knew it.

The woman clucked to her horses and pulled them to a stop on the outskirts of the crowd, climbing down from the coach with no trouble. The process was a bit more complicated for Ella, but it wasn't until the woman came around and took her arm and began to lead her into the crowd that Ella realized no one was paying them any attention. Perhaps the strange woman was a regular in town, and no one bothered being surprised by the coach or her anymore? It was almost like no one could see them…

She was so intent on the townspeople's reaction—or lack of reaction—to her, that she didn't even notice when the woman pulled her to a stop beside the bandstand. The Mayor was still speaking, but the woman leaned in close to her and patted her arm. She whispered, "Now you just wait here, my dear, and everything will be all right."

And then the Mayor was speaking to her, and when Ella glanced around in confusion, the woman had disappeared into the crowd, and she had no choice but to take Mr. Smith's offered hand and step up onto the bandstand.

The parade had been nice; Ian had sat with Ox and Gaston and Max in front of the Gingerbread House and hollered encouragement to the cowboys and their shows of trick riding. They'd all ribbed Max about not being up there with his brother, and his good-natured grin had hidden just a hint of envy. Then they'd ogled the ladies in their pretty dresses, and followed their noses to the fair grounds and the picnic that was being laid out. Ian had never felt more a part of something than he had today.

Now, he and Max were standing in the back of the crowd that clustered around the bandstand. The mayor had welcomed everyone and reminded everyone that the money raised from bidding on the picnic baskets would go — this year — to fix *Abuela* Zapato's orphanage roof. Then he'd invited the young ladies to form a line, and had begun to show off the picnic baskets.

The bidding on the baskets belonging to Rose and Snow, and Euna Smith and Ani Dokter, was fierce, and then it was the Miller sisters' turns. Gaston won the bidding on Eunice's basket, and strutted off beaming to collect his lunch companion. When Mr. Smith announced that Mabel's basket contained fried chicken, Ian had been half-tempted to bid on it himself, but decided that he'd rather keep the memory of Ella's meal untarnished. Nothing could compare to her fried chicken. Once the contents of the basket were announced, Mabel's bidding increased, and she lost her worried expression.

Ian elbowed Max and suggested that he join the fray, but his friend's tight-lipped head-shake told him that he didn't want anything to do with the Miller sisters. That didn't stop Ian from ribbing his new friend, though, throughout the basket bidding. Ox and Ian did their best to sell their friend on each subsequent lady's basket, until he finally threw up his hands.

"Why don't *you* bid, Ian? Still waiting for your mystery lady?"

Waiting, indeed. She wouldn't be here today, but that didn't matter. He'd seen her last night, touched her, and gotten her promise that she'd be back. He *would* see her again.

So he just smiled, and dipped his chin in agreement. "That's right. No one here can come close to her." It was the truth. She was beyond compare.

The line of eligible ladies grew shorter and shorter, and the crowd thinned out as men "won" the pleasure of the ladies' company, until the Mayor began to thank everyone for coming and announcing the total collected. It was a significant amount, and when Ian joined in the cheering, he really felt like he'd found someplace to belong.

But then the Mayor held up his hands, shushing them, and was saying something about one last entry. He reached out his hand, and pulled a young lady up on stage, and Ian felt his heart stop.

"*Hoooooooooboy.*" Ian found himself nodding in agreement with Ox's approving whistle. She was... stunning wasn't the right word. She was a vision. His Ella was up there on the bandstand, dressed in a gown that perfectly matched her eyes, those gorgeous curls falling down her back like they always did in his dreams, looking not a little confused. She was… She was perfect.

He willed her to find him in the crowd, and judging from the way her eyes darted here and there, she was trying. The Mayor asked her a question, gesturing at the bundle that dangled from one of her hands, and had to repeat it twice to get her answer. Finally, Ian saw her whisper something, and Mr. Smith turned back to the crowd.

"Ladies and gentlemen, we have one last young lady, who hasn't given her name. Her basket contains oatmeal cookies, apparently." He cleared his throat, no doubt puzzled by her offering. "What will you give me for them? What will you give me for what I assume are delicious cookies, and the company of this fair young vision?"

Everything.

It wasn't until Max asked him to repeat it that Ian realized he'd said it aloud. So he smiled, lifted his chin, and raised his voice. "Absolutely everything."

The crowd shifted and murmured in response to his bold claim, and the people closest to him turned. Ian didn't care though; he had eyes only for Ella, who'd finally found him among all the others. As he fitted his crutch under his right arm, and began to move through the crowd, everyone backed away, forming a path directly to her. She wasn't smiling when she took a tentative step towards the edge of the bandstand closest to him, but he didn't mind. He was coming for her.

He held her gaze as he hobbled towards her, keeping those gorgeous turquoise eyes on his by sheer willpower alone. She didn't blink, and he tried to tell her that everything would be all right. They'd be together.

They reached the edge of the bandstand at the same time. Ian halted, looking up at her, and realized that she was holding her breath, the same as he was. He placed the crutch on the rough wood planking, and hitched his right knee up to brace on top of the structure. He wanted to take her in his arms, to show all of Everland that she was his, and was going to be his forever.

But the Mayor moved closer, holding out the collection box. Without breaking eye contact with her, Ian dug into his right trouser pocket and pulled out all of the coins he was carrying. He wasn't sure exactly how much was there—probably not more than ten dollars. But if the Mayor needed more, he'd get it. Ian would give everything to spend the day with her.

Absolutely everything.

The *clink* of the coins in the collection box just barely registered, and the looming presence of Mr. Smith backed away, and there were only two people in the universe again. Ian found himself tensing, poised, waiting for a sign from her to tell him that this was *right*, this was what she wanted.

She touched him. Standing there, above him, she reached out one beautifully callused set of fingers and brushed the hair off of his forehead. The simple gesture shot sparks across his skin and through his soul, and he was lost. It was the only motivation he needed.

Putting his weight on the knee that was braced against the bandstand, Ian wrapped his hands around her tiny waist, and lifted her down to stand beside him. When he first moved, she gasped, and grabbed at his upper arms; even when she was standing safely beside him, her touch lingered, and Ian found himself hoping she'd never stop.

They stood, staring at one another, for a long moment. He knew that they were being watched, that there were people all around — people whom he'd come to care about, people who'd accepted him as part of Everland. But at that moment, none of them mattered more than this woman.

"You came."

Her smile was sweet, and when she lifted her fingertips to caress his cheek, he didn't see any of the hesitation he'd seen the night before in her eyes. She'd come. She was here, with him. "I promised you."

When her hand fluttered across his jaw, Ian's control vanished. He grabbed her hand and brought it to his lips, pressing a kiss against her palm. It wasn't where he'd been dreaming of tasting her, but it was close enough. And judging from the way she closed her eyes on a shudder, she felt their connection as well. Her voice was rough, hoarse, when she admitted, "…I just didn't expect to join in the basket auction."

He answered truthfully. "I'm glad that you did, Ella. I've been looking for you for weeks. My friends were beginning to think that I'd made you up, but when you showed up here, looking like a princess…" He would be the envy of half of Everland's population.

When she opened her eyes again, there was a hint of uncertainty. "I'm sorry about my basket, though."

"What about it?"

"I was so busy packing my sisters' baskets that I didn't think to pack one for myself. So all I have to offer you for your contribution is cookies."

When she began to chew on her bottom lip in concern, he couldn't stop from staring at it. In his dreams, he'd been the one to nibble on that lip, and he wasn't going to last much longer without tasting it. "Sweetheart, I love oatmeal cookies." It wasn't a lie; they'd been his mother's specialty.

"But I'm sorry. You'll want more than…" His expression must've changed, because she suddenly went all flustered and trailed off. She cleared her throat and looked away.

"Yeah," he drawled, and vaguely heard whistles from the crowd.

He cupped her cheek, turning her face, her lips back towards him. He knew his grin turned wicked, and loved the way her eyes widened as she understood. Her whisper seemed distracted. "I'm not particularly hungry."

"I am."

She exhaled slightly at his growled promise, and then he was finally tasting her. She wrapped her arms around his neck, he pulled her close enough to him to feel the length of her, and he was gone.

Kissing Ella was everything that he dreamed it would be. She was sweet, she was hot, she was *Ella*. She tasted of rightness, of home, of a future. Her fingers twined through the hair at the base of his neck, and her breasts pushed against his chest through the silk of her dress and the cotton of his suit, and he didn't know how he was going to restrain himself from peeling the gown off of her. *God*, she tasted good.

She tasted *right*.

She was his.

When they finally broke apart, each gasping for air, the cheers of the crowd — of his friends, his home — registered. Keeping one arm around her waist — not sure that he could let her go now — he turned away from the bandstand and adjusted his spectacles. Were they foggy, or was that his imagination?

He met Max's eyes across the crowd, and his friend's smile and nod of approval made Ian puff up a bit. Other men in the crowd were still hooting and hollering, and more than one woman was fanning herself frantically. Hank Cutter had his arms around his wife, and she was staring up at him with enough love in her expression to make sure everyone around them saw it.

And Ian knew that's what he wanted with Ella. He wanted to love her, to earn her love, and have everyone around them know it. Forever.

It was positively the most magical moment of Ella's life. The sensation of Ian's skin against hers, the taste of his lips, the feeling of his very *soul* pressed against hers… it was much, much better than her dreams. And when they pulled apart, she knew that she wanted to feel it again and again and again. She wanted to spend a night — many nights! All nights! — wrapped in his arms. She wanted to feel him peel her gown down her arms; she wanted to

wrap her fingers around his forearms and trace the
hills and valleys of his chest. She wanted *more*.

Who knew that wishing upon a star would
bring such grand results after all?

But the moment was marred when Ian turned
her to face the crowd, and she knew that everyone
was staring, wondering who she was. These were
people who'd lived near her for most of her life, and
she didn't know a single one of them; hadn't been
allowed to know a single one of them.

That wasn't true; she knew two of the
bystanders. Papa and Sibyl stood off to one side, and
Ella forced herself to meet their eyes. To her
complete astonishment, her stepfather showed no
signs of recognition. The cold fury she'd expected to
see just wasn't there; his ice-blue eyes showed
merely a distaste at what she assumed he considered
a disgusting display of affection.

Once Ella considered the situation, she
realized that she shouldn't be surprised; Papa had
never really *seen* her; he'd never considered her one
of his daughters, had never looked at her for more
than the moment it took to assign a new chore or
dole out a punishment on behalf of one of her sisters.
Now, garbed in a gorgeously expensive gown, with
her "disgusting Gypsy" hair down for the world to
see—against his dictates—he didn't even recognize
her.

It was that moment that Ella knew that Papa
didn't represent her future. If he couldn't see her—
really *see* her—then he didn't deserve her.

Beside him, Sibyl was wearing the delighted
grin that meant she couldn't believe what was
happening, and was excited to see the outcome. She
definitely recognized her older stepsister, and Ella

wondered if she'd fess up. She lifted her chin, deciding that she didn't care if Sibyl did her worst... but then Sibyl's expression softened, and she glanced up at her father and drew his attention by pointing towards something on the far side of the field. Ella vowed that she'd find a way to thank this youngest stepsister of hers, once she got back home.

No, back to the *ranch*; the Miller Ranch had never been a home to her. It had been a prison. Ella dismissed her stepfather, and glanced up at Ian, who was looking thoughtful. *This* was her home; wherever Ian was. He was her heart.

"How many stepsisters did you say that you had?"

It was an odd question, especially after what they'd shared, and Ella answered it without wondering. "Three."

"Hmmmmm," was all he said, but she saw his mind working. She didn't want to spend her one day of freedom discussing her past, though. She wanted to spend it with him, loving him. Showing him what things could be like, if she ever was able to break free from her stepfather.

But Papa's threat still hung over them. He was a powerful man, and unless Ian had gained some standing in the community since Edmund Miller made the ultimatum, it was a real concern; Papa could end him, could ruin his business, could drive him out of town. Ella wasn't going to let that happen. She loved Ian, and she wasn't going to let her stepfather ruin his hard work. As much as she was coming to realize that her future was with him, she would go back to the ranch and sacrifice that future, if it meant Ian's safety.

For now, though, she had him. She had a new gown, she had new shoes, she had a lovely day, and she had him. She'd celebrate Independence Day; independence from her family and from responsibility. Tonight, she'd sneak back home before Papa and the girls did — Ella squeezed up against Ian and made a vow to watch her family, to make sure that she left before them — but for now, she was free.

When she met Ian's gaze again, he was smiling, and she couldn't help but smile back. He bent to pick up his crutch, and she begrudged the few moments of movement that meant he wasn't holding her. Remedying that, he tucked her up against him once more, and Ella sighed in contentment. "Come on, sweetheart."

No one had called her "sweetheart" since her mother had passed away. The endearment caused her heart to swell with happiness. She was where she belonged, with him.

Now, if only she could figure out how to convince her family of this. Convince them to let her go, to be with Ian. Convince *him* that she was the one who'd love him forever, just the way he was. Convince herself that they deserved a future.

He led her towards the shade of a tall birch, and pulled her down to the grass with him. And the rest of the afternoon continued to be magical, too.

CHAPTER TEN

Yesterday had been… magical. Ian stacked his hands behind his head, reveling in the way the breeze from the open window cooled his heated skin, and relived every moment of yesterday's picnic. He still couldn't believe that she'd come — didn't know how she'd managed that. But he'd known then, when he claimed her in front of all of Everland, that she'd be his. He was going to ask her to marry him, and he'd make sure that she spent the rest of her life knowing how important and valued she was. She'd never again slave away for her family.

After the spectacle at the bandstand, they'd spent the afternoon on a little grassy rise under that birch tree. They'd fed each other cookies and other delicious food — Ella did leave briefly to fill up two plates with barbequed pork and salads and cornbread — and talked for long hours. They'd discussed the pup's health, and how she'd be up playing with Manny in no time. She told him about the peculiar woman who'd come to her ranch — she didn't even notice that she'd given him that clue to her family — and brought her the lovely dress. The stranger had disappeared right before the basket auction, and

Ian agreed that she sounded like the mysterious stranger who he'd been hearing about over the last year.

He'd told her about his past, and about how hard he'd worked to make it here to Everland. He'd told her how he'd found a place here in town, only recently, thanks to new friends like Max DeVille and Hank Cutter. He'd told her how he'd found a place to belong, and how he'd help her make new friends.

And he touched her as often as possible. Even when they weren't kissing, he'd been holding her hand, or she was running her fingers through his hair. They couldn't seem to not be in contact, and he loved it. He loved everything about her.

Despite the fact that no one was around them, Ian had known that they weren't alone. The people of Everland were watching them constantly, and he welcomed their interest. He was going to marry this woman, after all. As the sun dipped lower in the west, the band started up again, and the couples came together to dance. Ian pulled his crutch towards him to escort her towards the dancing, but she stopped him with her hand over his.

Meeting her clear eyes, he held his breath. "No," she'd said. "No. I want to stay here with you."

Ian had felt his heart trying to climb up his throat. Loved everything about her? No, he loved *her*. She didn't pity him, but accepted his limitations. She accepted him as he was, and he loved her for it.

When it was nearly dark, she'd kissed him one last time — that kiss! — and looked into his eyes. "Ian Crowne, I love you." He thought his heart would explode.

And then, while he was still trying to make himself breathe again, she turned and disappeared into the crowd. He hadn't been able to find her again. She'd disappeared, just like that first time.

Only now, he knew she was real. Knew she was his. How could she not be, if she loved him? And after seeing the way she'd peered at the bystanders at the basket auction, he had a fairly good idea who she was.

And there were a pair of cowboy boots downstairs that needed returning.

Yesterday had been magical, but today…? Ian smiled up at the ceiling, knowing that last night's dreams couldn't compare to yesterday's kisses. Today was going to be the start of their future.

"And that dress! Did you see how lovely that turquoise silk and velvet went together?"

"Oh, the cut was just divine! Wasn't it just divine, Sibyl? Of course, with you dragging us around to talk to people, I only ever got to see the backside of the dress. Did you see the front, Eunice?"

"No, Gaston kept me busy feeding him pasta salad and cookies. He's a man after my own heart."

Mabel huffed and rolled her eyes. "Sibyl, since you must have seen it, do sketch it for Ella. I want a dress like that, in red for next year."

As their youngest sister muttered something noncommittal and glanced in her direction, Ella ducked her head over her pot roast, and tried to hide her smile. She kept having to remind herself that as far as her older stepsisters were concerned, she'd spent yesterday here at the ranch, definitely not enjoying herself or practicing kissing with Everland's most handsome bachelor.

Normally, she'd be thrilled to listen to Mabel and Eunice relate every detail of the July Fourth celebration; hanging on each word and hoping against hope that they'd tell how they each managed to snag a husband with her gowns or her cooking. That had been Ella's goal for so long, it was odd to realize that yesterday was the culmination of all of her work.

But today, it had been hard to listen to them go on and on about how wonderful the parade and picnic and dancing had been, inflating their experiences and preening in front of her, knowing that she could reveal that *she'd been there*. She'd sat on the hill and watched the dancing with Ian, and knew that while Eunice had danced every song with Ian's friend Gaston, Mabel had pouted and sulked through a few partners, and then sat alone and fumed most of the time.

Yesterday had been magical, but had been far too public. With Papa's threat hanging over her head, she knew that, if she wanted to see Ian again, it'd have to be in private. Could she spend the rest of her life sneaking away to see him? Or could she be strong enough to defy her stepfather's edict, to risk his wrath, to be with Ian? Could they thwart him, together?

"She had the loveliest dress—far nicer than anything *Ella* could manage for us, that's certain." Mabel was being nasty, as usual. "Daddy, could you send away for some Paris magazines again? Maybe Ella could manage something half that nice, if she practiced some more."

Papa was reading his newspaper, as usual, and gave a distracted "Yes, darling" before flipping the page. Mabel smirked, and the birds sitting on the bush outside the dining room window began to chirp and trill again. The oldest Miller daughter sent them a dark look, and Ella managed not to roll her eyes. Apparently, she wasn't the only one who found the birds' attention annoying.

Eunice reached for the mashed potatoes, and Ella eyed her gown with a bit of worry, wondering if she was going to have to take out her sister's dresses if she kept eating like this. "Well, her dress was lovely, but so was her suitor."

"Oh, I *know*." Mabel's smitten sigh dragged Ella's attention away from the mound of potatoes on Eunice's plate. "That man might be a cripple, but did you *see* his arms?"

Eunice pretended to fan herself with her fork. "Be still, my heart. Freckles and red hair have suddenly become quite suitable. And those eyes? I never knew a pair of spectacles could be so *manly*, but the way he looked at her…" Both she and Mabel sighed in unison. "She must be *quite* the hussy, to have snagged him so quickly."

Ella felt the meat turn to lead in her stomach, and she put her fork down beside her plate. Knowing that she couldn't defend herself, defend him, was hard.

But to her surprise, salvation came from an unexpected source. "Well, Daddy and I watched the whole scene, and I thought that the kiss was incredibly romantic." Ella looked across the table, and found Sibyl staring directly at her. "Mr. Crowne was obviously very much in love with her, and I think that she was in love with him, too." The birdsong suddenly seemed much louder than a moment before.

Ella swallowed again, unable to answer the question in her younger stepsister's eyes. She wanted to thank Sibyl—for seeing, for understanding—and maybe someday she'd find a way. Not today, though. Not at Papa's table.

Speaking of whom… "What's that?" Apparently his name had drawn him back into the conversation. "You're talking about that Yankee in my house?"

Mabel was quick to dismiss his reaction. "We're just saying how handsome he is, Daddy. Now that he's joined society, and isn't hiding away in that shop of his, we've realized what a fine catch he'd be."

Slowly, deliberately, Papa creased his paper and placed it beside his plate. He folded his hands in front on him, leaned forward, and said, "Let me be clear." He met each girls' eyes in turn, including Ella's, whom he held. "You will not admire him. He is nothing." His voice rose in volume, but Ella refused to flinch. "He has found a hussy to keep him busy, and you will not mention his name again in this house. *Am I clear?*"

"I think that's going to be a problem, sir."

Ella had fainted in the face of her stepfather's anger, and was dreaming. That was the only explanation for why she was hearing Ian's voice here, in the dining room of the Miller Ranch. But she squeezed her eyes shut, and opened them again, and Papa was staring at the door like he'd seen a ghost. Unable to hope, Ella slowly turned in her chair.

He was real. *He was here*.

Ian took one of his hopping steps into the room, swinging himself on his crutch with the sheer strength of those massive shoulders, and Ella couldn't do a thing except stare. Maybe she *was* dreaming. But no; he caught her eye, and smiled, and she remembered the taste of those lips and knew that this was no dream.

This was better than a dream.

"Mr. Crowne!" Mabel's sickly-sweet voice cut through Ella's daze. "We were just speaking of you. Do come join us for dinner."

Without dropping Ella's gaze, he shook his head slightly. "No thank you, Miss Miller. I'll just be here a moment."

"How did you get into my house?" Her stepfather's croak sounded like he was just-barely containing his fury. "Where in the hell is Heyward?"

"Oh, he's... too slow."

Mr. Heyward chose that incredibly opportune moment to stagger through the doorway, slumping against the jamb. He had both hands clasped over his nose, and blood was dribbling from between his fingers. He met Papa's gaze, and groaned, and Ella finally felt a moment's pity for the man who followed her stepfather's every order. He'd obviously tried to stand up to Ian, but underestimated her prince's strength.

Ian winked at her, faintly, and Ella wondered if anyone else had seen it. But then he moved closer to the table, and looked her stepfather dead in the eye. "Mr. Heyward—who I recognize from hanging around outside my store, by the way—tried to stop me from entering. But I decided that I wasn't going to accept that answer."

"You *decided*?" Oh dear. Papa sounded like he was choking, and just as soon as Ella could make herself look away from the magnificent man standing beside the table, she'd check. "You think that it's okay, to just let yourself into a man's home?"

"I do, when that man is about to become my father-in-law."

There was silence for a long moment, and then the room erupted. Papa's incredulous roar mixed with Sibyl's excited squeal and her sisters' flattered clamorings.

Ian halted the racket without saying a word; he simply shifted slightly, and held up his other hand. There, dangling from the strong fingers she loved so well, were her boots, cleaned and oiled and gleaming. Her toes curled inside her new shoes, the ones that he'd gifted her, and knew that she'd be leaving with him today, somehow.

He spoke to them all, but it was Ella whose gaze he held. She couldn't — wouldn't — look away. "You see, Mr. Miller, I fell in love with one of your daughters a while ago. She's kind, and generous, and far more caring than the rest of her family. She's the type who'd defy you, just to save a puppy." Ella pushed away from the table slightly when he moved towards her, and she saw Mabel and Eunice exchange confused looks out of the corner of her eye. But it didn't matter — nothing mattered — because had he just announced his love for her? In front of her family? "I kissed her yesterday, for the first time, and knew that I couldn't let her escape me again."

Stopping beside her chair, he stared down at her in silence for a moment. No one spoke, and Ella fisted her hands in the lap, to keep from

reaching for him. She had to hear this. Had to
hear what he was going to say to her stepfather.
"The woman I love left me her boots." And then
he dropped to his knee, steadying himself against
the table leg. Their gazes were level, and she
could see every freckle, every thought behind his
glasses. She could see that he was holding his
breath, the same as her.

And then, he lifted the boots. "I brought
your boots back, Miss Ella."

Nothing in the whole world—not Mabel's
nasty "Well, I *never*" or her stepfather's bluster of
displeasure—could've stopped her from lifting
the hem of her faded blue dress, and letting him
slip the black shoes from her feet. When she sat
there, stocking toes pressed hard against the
wood floor, he moved the boots closer. Still
holding his pale green gaze, she pushed her feet
into her favorite old boots.

"They fit perfectly."

Her whisper only set her family off again,
but she didn't care. Their anger didn't matter.
Nothing did, except the way his grin threatened
to knock off his spectacles, and the love she saw
in his eyes.

Bracing himself on the table, he lifted
himself to his feet, and pulled her up as well. He
wrapped his arms around her, and pressed their
bodies together, and the birds sang stupidly, and
Ella knew that this was where she belonged. She
snaked her hands between his vest and his jacket,
reveling in the strength she felt under the cotton.
"I love you, Ian Crowne." He smiled, and she had

to confess why she'd withheld the truth for so long. "But my stepfather is a powerful man, and told me that he could ruin you, if I defied him."

Ian's grin faded, but not the love in his expression. After nearly a minute of staring down at her, he turned, pulling them both to face her stepfather. Edmund Miller was standing now, his hands braced on either side of his plate, his face red with fury. Slowly, he lifted one finger until it pointed directly at Ian's chest. "*You*. You think you're taking her away from here? You think to deprive me of her labor? I will *end you*, boy. I know how reclusive you are. I know that you don't have nearly the standing that I do, in this town. I'll make sure no one buys from you again. I'll make sure that your business will fail and you'll run back to the North where you belong."

The hatred she heard in Papa's voice was enough to make Ella blanch, but Ian just pulled her closer to him, as if to tell her that he'd keep her safe. He stared at her stepfather for a long moment, and then cocked his head to one side. "No. No, I don't think so."

His calm response confused Papa. He sucked in a breath, and began to cough. Ian's expression was grim when he continued. "You see, I'm part of this town, now. I've heard about you from Max DeVille, and I think that the people of this town respect me just as much as I do them, now. I think that any power you had over me disappeared the moment I began to look towards my future here, among them. Max has supported me, and — as you say — his family is important in

Everland. Everyone in town knows why I came out here today, and they support me. I'm marrying Ella, and taking her away from here. Away from you."

It was probably the most wonderful thing that she'd ever heard, and as soon as she could find her voice, she'd tell him that. For now, though, she just squeezed him as hard as she could. He glanced back down at her, as if her stepfather's sputtered threats — interspersed with coughing — meant nothing. "Yesterday, you didn't ask me what I named the dog."

"The…?" She'd almost forgotten about the reason she'd defied her stepfather to go to Ian two nights ago. "You've chosen a name?"

He nodded, his expression serious. "Future." *Future.* "You told me to stop living in the past, Ella, so I did. I've made a place for myself, for us. You gave me hope for the future, and I'm going to share it with you."

"It's… it's fitting." His shoulders dropped slightly, like he'd been holding his breath, waiting for her answer. "I think that Future will be quite happy with you, and Shiloh and Manny and Vick." And then she gave him the answer she knew he'd been waiting for. "And me."

He kissed her. There, in her stepfather's dining room, not caring about Papa's bluster or her sisters' squeals or Eunice's "Wait, that was *Ella* at the picnic yesterday?" He kissed her.

And Ella kissed him back, and never regretted anything less.

When they pulled apart, Ian grinned down at her, and no one else mattered. "I've got my wagon out front, sweetheart. Do you have anything here that you want to bring with you?"

She glanced down at the new shoes beside her chair. "Actually, I'd like to get my new dress."

Had she thought he was grinning before? It was nothing compared to the joy in his expression now. "Good. Actually, I was hoping you'd say that. Because Hank and Rojita, and Mr. and Mrs. Spratt are meeting us at the church in an hour, and I'd rather hoped that you'd wear that gown again."

The church? She swallowed, and he must've seen the question in her eyes, because his grin turned teasing. "That is, if you don't mind marrying me immediately?"

The clamor began again, but Ella had eyes only for him. With no other way to show him the love, the joy in her heart, she reached her hands up around his neck, and pulled his head down to hers.

And there, in the ruins of her past, poised at the beginning of her future, she kissed her husband-to-be.

They were married that afternoon, and she spent her wedding night with him in their new home, and it was everything they'd dreamed it would be. The dogs made sure that they had little privacy, and things were bit a cramped, and she had some trouble adjusting to life as a mercantile-owner's wife, but it didn't matter, because they had each other.

And they lived
Happily Ever After.
The End.

If you've enjoyed Ella and Ian's fairy tale, I urge you to friend me on Facebook or follow me on Twitter; I frequently post fun bits of social history that I find while researching my latest book. Do you like reading historical westerns, and like hanging out with others who do too? Join us on the Pioneer Hearts Facebook page, where we have the most wonderful discussions, contests, and updates about new books!

The *Everland, Ever After* series is going to be so much fun! If you'd like to keep up with my stories, or read deleted scenes, or receive exclusive free books, sign up for my newsletter.

You can get started at:
www.CarolineLeeRomance.com

Reviews help other readers find books they'll love.
All feedback is read and appreciated.

ABOUT THE AUTHOR

Caroline Lee is what George R.R. Martin once described as a "gardener author"; she delights in "planting" lovable characters in interesting situations, and allowing them to "grow" their own stories. Often they draw the story along to completely unexpected--and wonderful!--places. She considers a story a success if she can re-read it and sigh dreamily... and she wishes the same for you.

A love of historical romance prompted Caroline to pursue her degrees in social history; her Master's Degree is in Comparative World History, which is the study of themes across history (for instance, 'domestication of animals throughout the world,' or 'childhood through history'). Her theme? You guessed it: Marriage throughout world history. Her favorite focus was periods of history that brought two disparate peoples together to marry, like marriage in the Levant during the Kingdom of Jerusalem, or marriage between convicts in colonial New South Wales. She hopes that she's able to bring this love of history-- and this history of love-- to her novels.

Caroline is living her own little Happily Ever After with her husband and sons in North Carolina.

You can find her at
www.CarolineLeeRomance.com.

Made in the USA
Charleston, SC
13 May 2016